'Won't you take me to call on Mr Toad?' said the Mole. 'I've heard so much about him, and I do so want to make his acquaintance.' It was never the wrong time to call on Toad, as Ratty explained. Good-tempered, affectionate Toad was always glad to see you. Though he wasn't the cleverest of animals – he could be boastful and conceited, too – Toad had some excellent qualities. He also had a great enthusiasm for things: in fact you never knew what new fad he would take up next! First it was boating, then a canary-yellow gipsy caravan took his fancy, but soon a much more exciting and dangerous hobby was to win Toad over: a brand-new motor-car!

That was when the real trouble started – trouble which was to lead to Toad Hall being overrun by a band of weasels and stoats from the Wild Wood. Luckily for Toad, his faithful friends Mole, Water Rat and Badger stood by him. Would their daring and exciting attempt to reclaim Toad's ancestral home succeed?

This new Young Puffin edition of Kenneth Grahame's classic story has been abridged especially for younger readers. It contains new illustrations by Margaret Gordon, which bring Grahame's characters to life in the most enchanting way.

Tales from
The Wind
in the Willows

Kenneth Grahame

Illustrated by Margaret Gordon

Puffin Books

Puffin Books, Penguin Books Ltd, Harmondsworth, Middlesex, England
Viking Penguin Inc., 40 West 23rd Street, New York, New York 10010, U.S.A.
Penguin Books Australia Ltd, Ringwood, Victoria, Australia
Penguin Books Canada Limited, 2801 John Street, Markham, Ontario, Canada L3R 1B4
Penguin Books (N.Z.) Ltd, 182–190 Wairau Road, Auckland 10, New Zealand

First published in full 1908
This abridged edition published in Puffin Books 1985
Reprinted 1985

Illustrations copyright © Margaret Gordon, 1985

Printed and bound in Great Britain by
Cox & Wyman Ltd, Reading

Contents

I

The River Bank

The Mole had been working very hard all the
morning, spring-cleaning his little home. First
with brooms, then with dusters; then on ladders
and steps and chairs, with a brush and a pail of
whitewash; till he had dust in his throat and eyes,
and splashes of whitewash all over his black fur,

and an aching back and weary arms. Spring was moving in the air above and in the earth below and suddenly he flung down his brush on the floor, said 'Bother!' and 'O blow!' and also 'Hang spring-cleaning!' and bolted out of the house without even waiting to put on his coat. He scrabbled and scratched and scraped, working busily with his little paws and muttering to himself, 'Up we go! Up we go!' till at last, pop! his snout came out into the sunlight, and he found himself rolling in the warm grass of a great meadow.

'This is fine!' he said to himself. 'This is better than whitewashing!' The sunshine struck hot on his fur, and the carol of happy birds fell on his dulled hearing almost like a shout. Hither and thither through the meadows he rambled busily, along the hedgerows, across the copses, finding everywhere birds building, flowers budding, leaves thrusting – everything happy, and progressive, and occupied. And instead of having an uneasy conscience pricking him and whispering 'Whitewash!' he somehow could only feel how jolly it was to be the only idle dog among all these busy citizens.

He thought his happiness was complete when, as he meandered aimlessly along, suddenly he stood by the edge of a full-fed river. Never in his life had he seen a river before. All was a-shake and a-shiver – glints and gleams and sparkles, rustle and swirl, chatter and bubble. The Mole was bewitched, entranced, fascinated. By the side of the river he trotted and, when tired at last, he sat on the bank.

As he sat on the grass and looked across the river, a dark hole in the bank opposite, just above the water's edge, caught his eye. Something bright and small seemed to twinkle down in the heart of it, vanish, then twinkle once more like a tiny star. But it could hardly be a star in such an unlikely situation, and it was too glittering and small for a glow-worm. Then, as he looked, it winked at him, and so declared itself to be an eye, and a small face began gradually to grow up round it, like a frame round a picture.

A brown little face, with whiskers.

A grave round face, with the same twinkle in its eye that had first attracted his notice.

Small neat ears and thick silky hair.

It was the Water Rat!

'Hullo, Mole!' said the Water Rat.

'Hullo, Rat!' said the Mole.

'Would you like to come over?' inquired the Rat presently.

'O, it's all very well to *talk*,' said the Mole, rather pettishly, he being new to a river and riverside life and its ways.

The Rat said nothing, but stooped and unfastened a rope and hauled on it, then lightly stepped into a little boat which the Mole had not observed. It was painted blue outside and white within, and was just the size for two animals, and the Mole's whole heart went out to it at once, even though he did not yet fully understand its uses.

The Rat sculled smartly across and made fast. Then he held up his fore-paw as the Mole stepped gingerly down. 'Lean on that!' he said. 'Now then, step lively!' and the Mole to his surprise and rapture found himself actually seated in the stern of a real boat.

'This has been a wonderful day!' said he, as the Rat shoved off and took to the sculls again. 'Do you know, I've never been in a boat before in all my life.'

'What?' cried the Rat, open-mouthed. 'Never been in a – you never – well, I – what have you been doing, then?'

'Is it so nice as all that?' asked the Mole shyly.

'Nice? It's the *only* thing,' said the Water Rat solemnly, as he leant forward for his stroke. 'Believe me, my young friend, there is *nothing* – absolutely nothing – half so much worth doing as simply messing about in boats. Simply messing,' he went on dreamily: 'messing – about – in – boats; messing –'

'Look ahead, Rat!' cried the Mole suddenly.

It was too late. The boat struck the bank full tilt. The dreamer, the joyous oarsman, lay on his back at the bottom of the boat, his heels in the air.

'– about in boats – or *with* boats,' the Rat went on composedly, picking himself up with a pleasant laugh. 'In or out of 'em, it doesn't matter. Nothing seems really to matter, that's the charm of it. Whether you get away, or whether you don't; whether you arrive at your destination or whether you reach somewhere else, or whether you never get anywhere at all, you're always busy, and you never do anything in particular; and when you've done it there's always something else to do, and you can do it if you like, but you'd much better not. Look here! If you've really nothing else on hand this morning, supposing we drop down the river together, and have a long day of it?'

The Mole waggled his toes from sheer happiness and leaned back blissfully into the soft cushions. '*What* a day I'm having!' he said. 'Let us start at once!'

'Hold hard a minute, then!' said the Rat. He looped the painter through a ring in his landing-stage, climbed up into his hole above, and after a short interval reappeared staggering under a fat, wicker luncheon-basket.

'Shove that under your feet,' he observed to the Mole, as he passed it down into the boat. Then he untied the painter and took the sculls again.

'What's inside it?' asked the Mole, wriggling with curiosity.

'There's cold chicken inside it,' replied the Rat briefly; 'coldtonguecoldhamcoldbeefpickled gherkinssaladfrenchrollscresssandwidgespotted meatgingerbeerlemonadesodawater –'

'O stop, stop,' cried the Mole in ecstasies, 'this is too much!'

'Do you really think so?' inquired the Rat seriously. 'It's only what I always take on these little excursions, and the other animals are always telling me that I'm a mean beast and cut it *very* fine!'

The Mole never heard a word he was saying. Absorbed in the new life he was entering upon, intoxicated with the sparkle, the ripple, the scents and the sounds and the sunlight, he trailed a paw in the water and dreamed long waking dreams.

'So – this – is – a – River!' he said.

'*The* River,' corrected the Rat.

'And you really live by the river? What a jolly life!'

'By it and with it and on it and in it,' said the Rat. 'It's brother and sister to me, and aunts, and company, and food and drink, and (naturally) washing. It's my world, and I don't want any other. What it hasn't got is not worth having, and what it doesn't know is not worth knowing.'

'But isn't it a bit dull at times?' the Mole

ventured to ask. 'Just you and the river, and no one else to pass a word with?'

'No one else to – well, I mustn't be hard on you,' said the Rat with forbearance. 'You're new to it, and of course you don't know. The bank is so crowded nowadays that many people are moving away altogether. O no, it isn't what it used to be, at all. Otters, kingfishers, dabchicks, moorhens, all of them about all day long and always wanting you to *do* something – as if a fellow had no business of his own to attend to!'

'What lies over *there*?' asked the Mole, waving a paw towards a background of woodland that darkly framed the water-meadows on one side of the river.

'That? O, that's just the Wild Wood,' said the Rat shortly. 'We don't go there very much, we river-bankers.'

'Aren't they – aren't they very *nice* people in there?' said the Mole a trifle nervously.

'W-e-ll,' replied the Rat, 'let me see. The squirrels are all right. *And* the rabbits – some of 'em, but rabbits are a mixed lot. And then there's Badger, of course. He lives right in the heart of it; wouldn't live anywhere else, either, if you paid him to do it. Dear old Badger! Nobody interferes with *him*. They'd better not,' he added significantly.

'Why, who *should* interfere with him?' asked the Mole.

'Well, of course – there – are others,' explained the Rat in a hesitating sort of way. 'Weasels – and stoats – and foxes – and so on. They're all right in a way – I'm very good friends with them – pass the time of day when we meet, and all that – but you can't really trust them, and that's the fact.'

'And beyond the Wild Wood again?' asked the Mole.

'Beyond the Wild Wood comes the Wide World,' said the Rat. 'I've never been there, and I'm never going, nor you either, if you've got any sense at all. Now then! Here's where we're going to lunch.'

The Rat brought the boat alongside the bank, made her fast, helped the still awkward Mole safely ashore, and swung out the luncheon-basket. The Mole begged to be allowed to un-pack it all by himself; and the Rat was very pleased to sprawl at full length on the grass and rest, while his excited friend shook out the table-cloth and spread it, took out all the mysterious packets one by one and arranged their contents in due order, still gasping, 'O my! O my!' at each fresh revelation. When all was ready, the Rat said, 'Now, pitch in, old fellow!' and the Mole was indeed very glad to obey, for he had started

16

his spring-cleaning at a very early hour that morning and he had been through a very great deal since that distant time.

'What are you looking at?' said the Rat presently, when the edge of their hunger was somewhat dulled, and the Mole's eyes were able to wander off the table-cloth a little.

'I am looking,' said the Mole, 'at a streak of bubbles that I see travelling along the surface of the water. That is a thing that strikes me as funny.'

'Bubbles? Oho!' said the Rat, and chirruped cheerily in an inviting sort of way.

A broad glistening muzzle showed itself above the edge of the bank, and the Otter hauled himself out and shook the water from his coat.

'Greedy beggars!' he observed, making for the provender. 'Why didn't you invite me, Ratty?'

'This was an impromptu affair,' explained the Rat. 'By the way – my friend, Mr Mole.'

'Proud, I'm sure,' said the Otter, and the two animals were friends forthwith.

'Such a rumpus everywhere!' continued the Otter. 'All the world seems out on the river today. I came up this backwater to try and get a moment's peace, and then stumble upon you fellows! At least – I beg pardon – I don't exactly mean that, you know.'

There was a rustle behind them, proceeding from a hedge wherein last year's leaves still clung thick, and a stripy head, with high shoulders behind it, peered forth on them.

'Come on, old Badger!' shouted the Rat.

The Badger trotted forward a pace or two; then grunted, 'H'm! Company,' and turned his back and disappeared from view.

'That's *just* the sort of fellow he is!' observed the disappointed Rat. 'Simply hates Society! Now we shan't see any more of him today. Well, tell us *who*'s out on the river?'

'Toad's out, for one. In his brand-new wager-boat; new togs, new everything!'

The two animals looked at each other and laughed.

'Once, it was nothing but sailing,' said the Rat. 'Then he tired of that and took to punting. Nothing would please him but to punt all day and every day, and a nice mess he made of it. Last year it was house-boating, and we all had to go and stay with him in his house-boat, and pretend we liked it. He was going to spend the rest of his life in a house-boat. It's all the same, whatever he takes up; he gets tired of it, and starts on something fresh.'

'Such a good fellow, too,' remarked the Otter, and dived suddenly into the river again.

The Mole looked down. The voice was still in his ears, but the turf whereon he had sprawled was clearly vacant. Not an Otter to be seen, as far as the distant horizon, but again there was a streak of bubbles on the surface of the river.

'Well, well,' said the Rat, 'I suppose we ought to be moving. I wonder which of us had better pack the luncheon-basket?'

'O, please let me,' said the Mole. So, of course, the Rat let him.

Packing the basket was not quite such pleasant work as unpacking the basket. It never is. But the Mole was bent on enjoying everything, and although just when he had got the basket packed and strapped up tightly he saw a plate staring up at him from the grass, and when the job had been done again the Rat pointed out a fork which anybody ought to have seen, and last of all, behold! the mustard-pot, which he had been sitting on without knowing it – still, somehow, the thing got finished at last, without much loss of temper.

The afternoon sun was getting low as the Rat sculled gently homewards in a dreamy mood, murmuring poetry-things over to himself, and not paying much attention to Mole. But the Mole was very full of lunch and already quite at home in a boat (so he thought) and was getting a bit restless besides: and presently he said, 'Ratty! Please, *I* want to row, now!'

The Rat shook his head with a smile. 'Not yet, my young friend,' he said, 'wait till you've had a few lessons. It's not so easy as it looks.'

The Mole was quiet for a minute or two. But he began to feel more and more jealous of Rat, sculling so easily along, and his pride began to whisper that he could do it every bit as well. He jumped up and seized the sculls, so suddenly, that the Rat was taken by surprise and fell backwards off his seat with his legs in the air for the second time, while the triumphant Mole took his place and grabbed the sculls with entire confidence.

'Stop it, you *silly* ass!' cried the Rat, from the bottom of the boat. 'You can't do it! You'll have us over!'

The Mole flung his sculls back with a flourish and made a great dig at the water. He missed the surface altogether, his legs flew up above his head, and he found himself lying on the top of the prostrate Rat. Greatly alarmed, he made a grab at the side of the boat, and the next moment – Sploosh!

Over went the boat, and he found himself struggling in the river.

O my, how cold the water was, and O, how *very* wet it felt. How it sang in his ears as he went down, down, down! How bright and welcome the sun looked as he rose to the surface coughing and spluttering! How black was his despair when he felt himself sinking again! Then a firm paw gripped him by the back of his neck. It was the Rat, and the Mole could feel him laughing.

The Rat got hold of a scull and shoved it under the Mole's arm; then he did the same by the other side of him and, swimming behind, propelled the

helpless animal to shore, hauled him out, and set him down on the bank, a squashy, pulpy lump of misery.

When the Rat had rubbed him down a bit, and wrung some of the wet out of him, he said, 'Now then, old fellow! Trot up and down the towing-path as hard as you can, till you're warm and dry again, while I dive for the luncheon-basket.'

So the dismal Mole, wet without and ashamed within, trotted about till he was fairly dry, while the Rat plunged into the water again, recovered the boat, righted her and made her fast, fetched his floating property to shore by degrees, and finally dived successfully for the luncheon-basket and struggled to land with it.

When all was ready for a start once more, the Mole, limp and dejected, took his seat in the stern of the boat; and as they set off, he said in a low voice, broken with emotion, 'Ratty, my generous friend! I am very sorry indeed for my foolish and ungrateful conduct. My heart quite fails me when I think how I might have lost that beautiful luncheon-basket. Indeed, I have been a complete ass, and I know it. Will you overlook it this once and forgive me, and let things go on as before?'

'That's all right, bless you!' responded the Rat cheerily. 'What's a little wet to a Water Rat? I'm more in the water than out of it most days. Don't you think any more about it; and, look here! I really think you had better come and stop with me for a little time. It's very plain and rough, you know, but I can make you comfortable. And I'll teach you to row, and to swim, and you'll soon be as handy on the water as any of us.'

The Mole was so touched by his kind manner of speaking that he could find no voice to answer him, and he had to brush away a tear or two with the back of his paw. But the Rat kindly looked in another direction, and presently the Mole's spirits revived again.

When they got home, the Rat made a bright fire in the parlour, and planted the Mole in an arm-chair in front of it, having fetched down a dressing-gown and slippers for him, and told him river stories till supper-time. Very thrilling stories they were, too, to an earth-dwelling animal like Mole. Supper was a most cheerful meal, but very shortly afterwards a terribly sleepy Mole had to be escorted upstairs to the best bedroom, where he soon laid his head on his pillow in great peace and contentment, knowing that his new-found friend the River was lapping the sill of his window.

2

The Open Road

'Ratty,' said the Mole suddenly, one bright summer morning, 'if you please, I want to ask you a favour.'

The Rat was sitting on the river bank, singing a little song he had just composed about his friends the ducks:

> All along the backwater,
> Through the rushes tall,
> Ducks are a-dabbling,
> Up tails all!
>
> Ducks' tails, drakes' tails,
> Yellow feet a-quiver,
> Yellow bills all out of sight
> Busy in the river!
>
> Slushy green undergrowth
> Where the roach swim –
> Here we keep our larder,
> Cool and full and dim.

Everyone for what he likes!
We like to be
Heads down, tails up,
Dabbling free!

High in the blue above
Swifts whirl and call,
We are down a-dabbling,
Up tails all!

'I don't know that I think so *very* much of that little song, Rat,' observed the Mole cautiously.

'Nor don't the ducks neither,' replied the Rat cheerfully. '"What *nonsense* it all is!" That's what the ducks say.'

'So it is, so it is,' said the Mole, with great heartiness.

'No, it isn't!' cried the Rat indignantly.

'Well then, it isn't, it isn't,' replied the Mole soothingly. 'But what I wanted to ask you was, won't you take me to call on Mr Toad? I've heard so much about him, and I do so want to make his acquaintance.'

'Why, certainly,' said the good-natured Rat. 'Get the boat out, and we'll paddle up there at once. It's never the wrong time to call on Toad. Early or late he's always the same fellow. Always good-tempered, always glad to see you, always sorry when you go!'

'He must be a very nice animal,' observed the Mole as he got into the boat and took the sculls, while the Rat settled himself comfortably in the stern.

'He is indeed the best of animals,' replied Rat. 'So simple, so good-natured, and so affectionate. Perhaps he's not very clever – we can't all be geniuses; and it may be that he is both boastful and conceited. But he has got some great qualities, has Toady.'

Rounding a bend in the river, they came in sight of a handsome, dignified old house of mellowed red brick, with well-kept lawns reaching down to the water's edge.

'There's Toad Hall,' said the Rat, 'and that creek on the left, where the notice-board says "Private. No landing allowed", leads to his boat-house, where we'll leave the boat.'

They glided up the creek, and the Mole shipped his sculls as they passed into the shadow of a large boat-house. Here they saw many handsome boats, slung from the crossbeams or hauled up on a slip, but none in the water, and the place had an unused and a deserted air.

The Rat looked around him. 'I understand,' said he. 'Boating is played out. He's tired of it, and done with it. I wonder what new fad he has taken up now? Come along and let's look him up. We shall hear all about it quite soon enough.'

They disembarked, and strolled across the gay flower-decked lawns in search of Toad, whom they presently happened upon resting in a wicker garden-chair, with a preoccupied expression of face, and a large map spread out on his knees.

'Hooray!' he cried, jumping up on seeing them, 'this is splendid!' He shook the paws of both of them warmly, never waiting for an introduction to the Mole. 'How *kind* of you!' he went on, dancing round them. 'I was just going to send a boat down the river for you, Ratty, with strict orders that you were to be fetched up here at once, whatever you were doing. You are the very animals I wanted. You've got to help me. It's most important!'

'It's about your rowing, I suppose,' said the Rat, with an innocent air. 'You're getting on fairly well, though you splash a good bit still.'

'O, pooh! Boating!' interrupted the Toad, in great disgust. 'Silly boyish amusement. I've given that up *long* ago. Sheer waste of time, that's what it is. It makes me downright sorry to see you fellows, who ought to know better, spending all your energies in that aimless manner. No, I've discovered the real thing, the only genuine occupation for a lifetime. Come with me, dear Ratty, and your amiable friend also, if he will be so very good, just as far as the stable-yard, and you shall see what you shall see!'

He led the way to the stable-yard accordingly, the Rat following with a most mistrustful expression, and there, drawn out of the coach-house into the open, they saw a gipsy caravan, shining with newness, painted a canary-yellow picked out with green, and red wheels.

'There you are!' cried the Toad. 'There's real life for you – the open road, the dusty highway, the heath, the common, the hedgerows, the rolling downs! Camps, villages, towns, cities! Here today, up and off to somewhere else tomorrow! Travel, change, interest, excitement! The whole world before you, and a horizon that's always changing! And mind, this is the very finest cart of its sort that was ever built, without any exception. Come inside and look at the arrangements. Planned 'em all myself, I did!'

The Mole was tremendously interested and excited, and followed him eagerly up the steps and into the interior of the caravan. The Rat only snorted and thrust his hands deep into his pockets, remaining where he was.

It was indeed very compact and comfortable. Little sleeping-bunks – a little table that folded up against the wall – a cooking-stove, lockers, bookshelves, a bird-cage with a bird in it; and pots, pans, jugs and kettles of every size and variety.

'All complete!' said the Toad triumphantly, pulling open a locker. 'You see – biscuits, potted lobster, sardines – everything you can possibly want. Soda-water here – baccy there – letter-paper, bacon, jam, cards and dominoes – you'll find,' he continued, as they descended the steps again, 'you'll find that nothing whatever has been forgotten, when we make our start this afternoon.'

'I beg your pardon,' said the Rat slowly, as he chewed a straw, 'but did I overhear you say something about "*we*", and "*start*", and "*this afternoon*"?'

'Now, you dear good old Ratty,' said Toad imploringly, 'I can't possibly manage without you, so please consider it settled, and don't argue – it's the one thing I can't stand. You surely don't mean to stick to your dull fusty old river all your life, and just live in a hole in a bank, and *boat*? I want to show you the world! I'm going to make an *animal* of you, my boy!'

'I don't care,' said the Rat doggedly. 'I'm not coming, and that's flat. And I *am* going to stick to my old river, *and* live in a hole, *and* boat, as I've always done. And what's more, Mole's going to stick to me and do as I do, aren't you, Mole?'

'Of course I am,' said the Mole loyally. 'I'll always stick to you, Rat, and what you say is to be – has got to be. All the same, it sounds as if it might have been – well, rather fun, you know!' he added wistfully, for he had fallen in love at first sight with the canary-coloured cart and all its little fitments.

The Rat saw what was passing in his mind, and wavered. He hated disappointing people, and he was fond of the Mole, and would do almost anything to oblige him. Toad was watching both of them closely.

'Come along in and have some lunch,' he said diplomatically, 'and we'll talk it over. We needn't decide anything in a hurry. Of course, *I* don't really care. I only want to give pleasure to you fellows. "Live for others!" That's my motto in life.'

During luncheon – which was excellent, of course, as everything at Toad Hall always was – the Toad simply let himself go, painting the prospects of the trip and the joys of the open life and the roadside in such glowing colours that the

Mole could hardly sit in his chair for excitement. Somehow, it soon seemed taken for granted by all three of them that the trip was a settled thing; and the Rat, though still unconvinced in his mind, allowed his good-nature to over-ride his personal objections. He could not bear to disappoint his two friends, who were already deep in schemes and anticipations, planning out each day's separate occupation for several weeks ahead.

When they were quite ready, the now triumphant Toad led his companions to the paddock and set them to capture the old grey horse, who, without having been consulted, and to his own extreme annoyance, had been told off by Toad for the dustiest job in this dusty expedition. He frankly preferred the paddock, and took a deal of catching. Meantime Toad packed the lockers still tighter with necessaries, and hung nose-bags, nets of onions, bundles of hay, and baskets from the bottom of the cart. At last the horse was caught and harnessed and they set off, all talking at once, each animal either trudging by the side of the cart or sitting on the shaft, as the humour took him. It was a golden afternoon. The smell of the dust they kicked up was rich and satisfying; out of thick orchards on either side the road, birds called and whistled to them cheerily; good-natured wayfarers, passing them, gave them 'Good day', or stopped to say nice things about their beautiful cart; and rabbits, sitting at their front doors in the hedgerows, held up their fore-paws, and said, 'O my! O my! O my!'

Late in the evening, tired and happy and miles from home, they drew up on a common, turned the horse loose to graze and ate their simple supper sitting on the grass by the side of the cart. Toad talked big about all he was going to do in the days to come, while stars grew fuller and

larger all around them, and a yellow moon,
appearing suddenly and silently from nowhere
in particular, came to keep them company and
listen to their talk. At last they turned into their
little bunks in the cart and Toad, kicking out his
legs, sleepily said, 'Well, good night, you fellows!
This is the real life for a gentleman! Talk about
your old river!'

'I *don't* talk about my river,' replied the
patient Rat. 'You *know* I don't, Toad. But I
think about it,' he added pathetically, in a lower
tone, 'I think about it – all the time!'

The Mole reached out from under his blanket,
felt for the Rat's paw in the darkness, and gave

it a squeeze. 'I'll do whatever you like, Ratty,' he whispered. 'Shall we run away tomorrow morning, quite early – *very* early – and go back to our dear old hole on the river?'

'No, no, we'll see it out,' whispered back the Rat. 'Thanks awfully, but I ought to stick by Toad till this trip is ended. It wouldn't be safe for him to be left to himself. It won't take very long. His fads never do. Good night!'

The end was indeed nearer than even the Rat suspected.

After so much open air and excitement the Toad slept very soundly, and no amount of shaking could rouse him out of bed next morning. So the Mole and the Rat turned to, quietly and manfully, and while the Rat saw to the horse, and lit a fire, and cleaned last night's cups and platters, and got things ready for breakfast, the Mole trudged off to the nearest village for milk and eggs and various necessaries the Toad had, of course, forgotten to provide. The hard work had all been done and the two animals were resting, thoroughly exhausted, by the time Toad appeared on the scene, fresh and gay, remarking what a pleasant easy life it was they were all leading now, after the cares and worries of housekeeping at home.

They had a pleasant ramble that day over grassy downs and along narrow by-lanes and camped, as before, on a common, only this time the two guests took care that Toad should do his fair share of work. In consequence, when the time came for starting next morning, Toad was by no means so rapturous about the simplicity of the primitive life and indeed attempted to resume his place in his bunk, whence he was hauled by force. Their way lay, as before, across country by narrow lanes, and it was not till the afternoon that they came out on their first high road; and there disaster sprang out on them.

They were strolling along the high road easily, the Mole by the horse's head, talking to him, and the Toad and the Water Rat walking behind the cart, when far behind them they heard a faint warning hum, like the drone of a distant bee. Glancing back, they saw a small cloud of dust, with a dark centre of energy, advancing on them at incredible speed, while from out of the dust wailed a faint 'poop-poop!' Hardly regarding it, they turned to resume their conversation, when in an instant (as it seemed) the peaceful scene was changed, and with a blast of wind and a whirl of sound that made them jump for the nearest ditch, it was on them! The 'poop-poop' rang with a brazen shout in their ears, they had a moment's glimpse of an interior of glittering plate-glass and rich morocco, and the magnificent motor-car, immense, breath-snatching, passionate, with its pilot tense and hugging his wheel, flung an enveloping cloud of dust that blinded and enwrapped them utterly, and then dwindled to a speck in the far distance.

The old grey horse, dreaming, as he plodded along, of his quiet paddock, in a new raw situation such as this simply abandoned himself to his natural emotions. Rearing, plunging, backing steadily, in spite of all the Mole's efforts at his head, he drove the cart backwards towards the deep ditch at the side of the road. It wavered an instant – then there was a heartrending crash – and the canary-coloured cart, their pride and their joy, lay on its side in the ditch, an irredeemable wreck.

The Rat danced up and down in the road, simply transported with passion. 'You villains!' he shouted, shaking both fists. 'You scoundrels, you highwaymen, you – you – road-hogs! – I'll have the law on you! I'll report you! I'll take you through all the Courts!'

Toad sat straight down in the middle of the dusty road, his legs stretched out before him, and stared fixedly in the direction of the disappearing motor-car. He breathed short, his face wore a placid, satisfied expression, and at intervals he faintly murmured 'poop-poop!'

The Mole was busy trying to quiet the horse, which he succeeded in doing after a time. Then he went to look at the cart, on its side in the ditch. It was indeed a sorry sight. Panels and windows smashed, axles hopelessly bent, one wheel off, sardine-tins scattered over the wide world, and the bird in the bird-cage sobbing pitifully and calling to be let out.

The Rat came to help him, but their united efforts were not sufficient to right the cart. 'Hi! Toad!' they cried. 'Come and bear a hand, can't you!'

The Toad never answered a word or budged from his seat in the road, so they went to see what was the matter with him. They found him in a sort of trance, a happy smile on his face, his eyes still fixed on the dusty wake of their destroyer. At intervals he was still heard to murmur 'poop-poop!'

The Rat shook him by the shoulder. 'Are you coming to help us, Toad?' he demanded sternly.

'Glorious, stirring sight!' murmured Toad, never offering to move. 'The *real* way to travel! The *only* way to travel! O bliss! O poop-poop! O my! O my!'

'O *stop* being an ass, Toad!' cried the Mole despairingly.

'And to think I never *knew*!' went on the Toad in a dreamy monotone. 'All those wasted years that lie behind me, I never knew, never even *dreamt*! But *now* – but now that I know, now that I fully realize! O what a flowery track lies spread before me, henceforth! What dust-clouds shall spring up behind me as I speed on my reckless way! What horrid little canary-coloured carts I shall fling carelessly into the ditch!

'I've done with carts for ever,' said Toad. 'I never want to see the cart or hear of it again,' and next morning he went on an early train to town, and he ordered a large and very expensive motor-car!

3

The Wild Wood

The Mole had long wanted to make the acquaintance of the Badger. But whenever he mentioned his wish to the Water Rat he always found himself put off. 'It's all right,' the Rat would say, 'Badger'll turn up some day or other – he's always turning up – and then I'll introduce you.'

'Couldn't you ask him here – dinner or something?' said the Mole.

'He wouldn't come,' replied the Rat simply. 'Badger hates invitations and dinner, and all that sort of thing.'

'Well, then, supposing we go and call on *him*?' suggested the Mole.

'O, I'm sure he wouldn't like that at *all*,' said the Rat, quite alarmed. 'He's so very shy, he'd be sure to be offended. I've never even ventured to call on him at his own home myself, though I know him so well. Besides, we can't. It's quite out of the question, because he lives in the very middle of the Wild Wood.'

'Well, supposing he does,' said the Mole. 'You told me the Wild Wood was all right, you know.'

'O, I know, I know, so it is,' replied the Rat evasively. 'But I think we won't go there just now. Not *just* yet. It's a long way, and he wouldn't be at home at this time of year anyhow, and he'll be coming along some day, if you'll wait quietly.'

The Mole had to be content with this. But the Badger never came along, and every day brought its amusements, and it was not till summer was over that he found his thoughts dwelling again with much persistence on the solitary grey Badger, who lived his own life by himself, in his hole in the middle of the Wild Wood.

In the winter time the Rat slept a great deal, retiring early and rising late. During his short day he sometimes scribbled poetry or did other small domestic jobs about the house and, of course, there were always animals dropping in for a chat.

There was plenty to talk about on those short

winter days when the animals found themselves round the fire, but the Mole still had a good deal of spare time on his hands, and so one afternoon, when the Rat in his arm-chair before the blaze was alternately dozing and trying over rhymes that wouldn't fit, he formed the resolution to go out by himself and explore the Wild Wood, and perhaps strike up an acquaintance with Mr Badger.

It was a cold still afternoon with a hard steely sky overhead, when he slipped out of the warm parlour into the open air. The country lay bare and entirely leafless around him, and with great cheerfulness of spirit he pushed on towards the Wild Wood.

There was nothing to alarm him at first entry. Twigs crackled under his feet, logs tripped him, funguses on stumps resembled caricatures and startled him for the moment by their likeness to something familiar and far away; but that was all fun, and exciting. It led him on, and he penetrated to where the light was less, and trees crouched nearer and nearer, and holes made ugly mouths at him on either side.

Everything was very still now. The dusk advanced on him steadily, rapidly, gathering in behind and before, and the light seemed to be draining away like flood-water.

Then the faces began.

It was over his shoulder, and indistinctly, that he first thought he saw a face: a little evil wedge-shaped face, looking out at him from a hole. When he turned and confronted it, the thing had vanished.

He quickened his pace, telling himself cheerfully not to begin imagining things, or there would be simply no end to it. He passed another hole, and another, and another, and then – yes! – no! – yes! Certainly a little narrow face, with hard eyes, had flashed up for an instant from a hole and was gone. He hesitated – braced himself up for an effort and strode on. Then suddenly, and as if it had been so all the time, every hole, far and near, seemed to possess its face, coming and going rapidly, all fixing on him glances of malice and hatred: all hard-eyed and evil and sharp.

If he could only get away from the holes in the banks, he thought, there would be no more faces. He swung off the path and plunged into the untrodden places of the wood.

Then the whistling began.

Very faint and shrill it was, and far behind him, when first he heard it, but somehow it made him hurry forward. Then, still very faint and shrill, it sounded far ahead of him, and made him hesitate and want to go back, for he was alone, and unarmed, and far from any help, and the night was closing in.

Then the pattering began.

He thought it was only falling leaves at first, so slight and delicate was the sound of it. Then as it grew it took a regular rhythm, and he knew it for nothing else but the pat-pat-pat of little feet, still a very long way off. Was it in front or behind? As he stood still to hearken, a rabbit came running hard towards him through the trees. He waited, expecting it to slacken pace, or to swerve from him into a different course. Instead, the animal almost brushed him as it dashed past, his face set and hard, his eyes staring. 'Get out of this, you fool, get out!' the Mole heard him mutter as he swung round a stump and disappeared down a friendly burrow.

The pattering increased till it sounded like sudden hail on the dry-leaf carpet spread around him. The whole wood seemed running now, running hard, hunting, chasing, closing in round somebody. In panic, he began to run too, aimlessly, he knew not whither. He ran up against things, he fell over things and into things, he darted under things and dodged round things. At last he took refuge in the dark deep hollow of an old beech tree and, as he lay there panting and trembling, and listened to the whistlings and the patterings outside, he knew it at last, that dread thing which other little dwellers in field and hedgerow had encountered here – the Terror of the Wild Wood!

Meantime the Rat, warm and comfortable, dozed by his fireside. His paper of half-finished verses slipped from his knee, his head fell back, his mouth opened, and he wandered by the verdant banks of dream-rivers. Then a coal slipped, the fire crackled and sent up a spurt of flame, and he woke with a start. He reached down to the floor for his verses and then looked round for the Mole to ask him if he knew a good rhyme for something or other.

But the Mole was not there.

He listened for a time. The house seemed very quiet.

Then he called 'Moly!' several times and, receiving no answer, got up and went out into the hall.

The Mole's cap was missing from its accustomed peg. His goloshes, which always lay by the umbrella-stand, were also gone.

The Rat left the house and carefully examined the muddy surface of the ground outside, hoping to find the Mole's tracks. There they were, sure enough. The goloshes were new, just bought for the winter, and the pimples on their soles were fresh and sharp. He could see the imprints of them in the mud, running along straight and purposeful, leading direct to the Wild Wood.

The Rat looked very grave, and stood in deep thought for a minute or two. Then he re-entered the house, strapped a belt round his waist, shoved a brace of pistols into it, took up a stout cudgel that stood in a corner of the hall, and set off for the Wild Wood.

It was already getting towards dusk when he reached the first fringe of trees and plunged without hesitation into the wood, looking anxiously on either side for any sign of his friend. Here and there wicked little faces popped out of holes, but vanished immediately at sight of the valorous

Rat, his pistols and the great ugly cudgel in his grasp. The whistling and pattering ceased and all was very still. He made his way manfully through the wood, laboriously working over the whole ground, and all the time calling out cheerfully, 'Moly, Moly, Moly! Where are you? It's me – it's old Rat!'

He had patiently hunted for an hour or more, when at last to his joy he heard a little answering cry. Guiding himself by the sound, he made his way through the gathering darkness to the foot of an old beech tree, with a hole in it, and from out of the hole came a feeble voice, saying, 'Ratty! Is that really you?'

The Rat crept into the hollow and there he found the Mole, exhausted and still trembling.

'O, Rat!' he cried, 'I've been so frightened, you can't think!'

'O, I quite understand,' said the Rat soothingly. 'You shouldn't really have gone and done it, Mole. I did my best to keep you from it. We river-bankers, we hardly ever come here by ourselves.'

'Surely the brave Mr Toad wouldn't mind coming here by himself, would he?' inquired the Mole.

'Old Toad?' said the Rat, laughing heartily. 'He wouldn't show his face here alone, not for a whole hatful of golden guineas, Toad wouldn't.'

The Mole was greatly cheered by the sound of the Rat's careless laughter, as well as by the sight of his stick and his gleaming pistols, and he stopped shivering and began to feel bolder and more himself again.

'Now then,' said the Rat presently, 'we really must pull ourselves together and make a start for home while there's still a little light left. It will never do to spend the night here.'

'Dear Ratty,' said the poor Mole, 'I'm dreadfully sorry, but I'm simply dead beat and that's a solid fact. You *must* let me rest here a while longer and get my strength back, if I'm to get home at all.'

'O, all right,' said the good-natured Rat, 'rest away. It's pretty nearly pitch dark now, anyhow, and there ought to be a bit of a moon later.'

So the Mole got well into the dry leaves and stretched himself out, and presently dropped off into sleep, though of a broken and troubled sort, while the Rat covered himself up, too, as best he might, for warmth, and lay patiently waiting, with a pistol in his paw.

When at last the Mole woke up, much refreshed and in his usual spirits, the Rat said, 'Now then! I'll just take a look outside and see if everything's quiet, and then we really must be off.'

He went to the entrance of their retreat and put his head out. Then the Mole heard him saying quietly to himself, 'Hullo! hullo! here – *is* – a – go!'

'What's up, Ratty?' asked the Mole.

'*Snow* is up,' replied the Rat briefly; 'or rather, *down*. It's snowing hard – Well, it can't be helped. We must make a start and take our chance. The worst of it is, I don't exactly know where we are. And now this snow makes everything look so very different.'

It did indeed. The Mole would not have known that it was the same wood. However, they set out bravely and took the line that seemed most promising.

An hour or two later, dispirited, weary, and hopelessly at sea, they sat down on a fallen tree-trunk to recover their breath and consider what was to be done. They were aching with fatigue and bruised with tumbles; they had fallen into several holes and got wet through; the snow was getting so deep that they could hardly drag their little legs through it, and the trees were thicker and more like each other than ever. There seemed to be no end to this wood, and no beginning, and no difference in it, and, worst of all, no way out.

'We can't sit here very long,' said the Rat. 'We shall have to make another push for it, and do something or other. The cold is too awful for anything, and the snow will soon be too deep for us to wade through.' He peered about him and considered. 'Look here,' he went on, 'this is what occurs to me. There's a sort of dell down there in front of us, where the ground seems all hilly and humpy and hummocky. We'll make our way down into that, and try and find some sort of shelter, a cave or hole with a dry floor to it, out of the snow and the wind, and there we'll have a good rest before we try again, for we're both of us pretty dead beat. Besides, the snow may leave off, or something may turn up.'

So once more they got on their feet and struggled down into the dell, where they hunted about for a cave or some corner that was dry and a protection from the keen wind and the whirling snow. They were investigating one of the hummocky bits the Rat had spoken of, when suddenly the Mole tripped up and fell forward on his face with a squeal.

'O, my leg!' he cried. 'O, my poor shin!' and he sat up on the snow and nursed his leg in both his front paws.

'Poor old Mole!' said the Rat kindly. 'You don't seem to be having much luck today, do you? Let's have a look at the leg. Yes,' he went on, going down on his knees to look, 'you've cut your shin, sure enough. Wait till I get at my handkerchief, and I'll tie it up for you.'

'I must have tripped over a hidden branch or a stump,' said the Mole miserably. 'O my! O my!'

'It's a very clean cut,' said the Rat, examining it again attentively. 'That was never done by a branch or a stump. Looks as if it was made by a sharp edge of something in metal. Funny!' He pondered a while, and examined the humps and slopes that surrounded them.

'Well, never mind what done it,' said the Mole, forgetting his grammar in his pain. 'It hurts just the same, whatever done it.'

But the Rat, after carefully tying up the leg with his handkerchief, had left him and was busy scraping in the snow. He scratched and shovelled and explored, all four legs working busily, while the Mole waited impatiently, remarking at intervals, 'O, *come* on, Rat!'

Suddenly the Rat cried 'Hooray!' and then 'Hooray-oo-ray-oo-ray-oo-ray!' and fell to executing a feeble jig in the snow.

'What *have* you found, Ratty?' asked the Mole, still nursing his leg.

'Come and see!' said the delighted Rat, as he jigged on.

The Mole hobbled up to the spot and had a good look.

'Well,' he said at last, slowly, 'I *see* it right enough. Seen the same sort of thing before, lots of times. A door-scraper! Well, what of it? Why dance jigs round a door-scraper?'

'But don't you see what it *means*, you – you dull-witted animal?' cried the Rat impatiently.

'Of course I see what it means,' replied the Mole. 'It simply means that some *very* careless and forgetful person has left his door-scraper lying about in the middle of the Wild Wood, *just* where it's *sure* to trip *everybody* up. Very thoughtless of him, I call it. When I get home I shall go and complain about it to – to somebody or other, see if I don't!'

'O dear! O dear!' cried the Rat, in despair at his obtuseness. 'Here, stop arguing and come and scrape!' And he set to work again and made the snow fly in all directions around him.

After some further toil his efforts were rewarded, and a very shabby door-mat lay exposed to view.

'There, what did I tell you?' exclaimed the Rat in great triumph.

'Absolutely nothing whatever,' replied the Mole, with perfect truthfulness. 'Well now,' he went on, 'you seem to have found another piece of domestic litter, done for and thrown away, and I suppose you're perfectly happy. Better go ahead and dance your jig round that if you've got to, and get it over, and then perhaps we can go on and not waste any more time over rubbish-heaps. Can we *eat* a door-mat? Or sleep under a door-mat? Or sit on a door-mat and sledge home on it, you exasperating rodent?'

'Do – you – mean – to – say,' cried the excited Rat, 'that this door-mat doesn't *tell* you any-thing?'

'Really, Rat,' said the Mole quite pettishly, 'I think we've had enough of this folly. Who ever heard of a door-mat *telling* anyone anything? They simply don't do it. They are not that sort at all. Door-mats know their place.'

'Now look here, you – you thick-headed beast,' replied the Rat, really angry, 'this must stop. Not another word, but scrape – scrape and scratch and dig and hunt round, especially on the sides of the hummocks, if you want to sleep dry and warm tonight, for it's our last chance!'

The Rat attacked a snow-bank beside them with ardour, probing with his cudgel everywhere and then digging with fury, and the Mole scraped busily too, more to oblige the Rat than for any other reason, for his opinion was that his friend was getting light-headed.

Some ten minutes' hard work, and the point of the Rat's cudgel struck something that sounded hollow. He worked till he could get a paw through and feel, then called the Mole to come and help him. Hard at it went the two animals, till at last the result of their labours stood full in view of the astonished and hitherto incredulous Mole.

In the side of what had seemed to be a snow-bank stood a solid-looking little door, painted a dark green. An iron bell-pull hung by the side, and below it, on a small brass plate, neatly engraved in square capital letters, they could read by the aid of moonlight:

MR BADGER

The Mole fell backwards on the snow from sheer surprise and delight. 'Rat!' he cried in penitence, 'you're a wonder! A real wonder,

that's what you are. I see it all now! You argued
it out, step by step, in that wise head of yours,
from the very moment that I fell and cut my shin,
and you looked at the cut, and at once your
majestic mind said to itself, "Door-scraper!"
And then you turned to and found the very door-
scraper that done it! Did you stop there? No.
Some people would have been quite satisfied, but
not you. Your intellect went on working. "Let
me only just find a door-mat," says you to
yourself, "and my theory is proved!" And of
course you found your door-mat. You're so
clever, I believe you could find anything you

liked. "Now," says you, "that door exists, as plain as if I saw it. There's nothing else remains to be done but to find it!" Well, I've read about that sort of thing in books, but I've never come across it before in real life. You ought to go where you'll be properly appreciated. You're simply wasted here, among us fellows. If I only had your head, Ratty –'

'But as you haven't,' interrupted the Rat rather unkindly, 'I suppose you're going to sit on the snow all night and *talk*? Get up at once and hang on to that bell-pull you see there, and ring hard, as hard as you can, while I hammer!'

4

Mr Badger

They waited patiently for what seemed a very long time, stamping in the snow to keep their feet warm. At last they heard the sound of slow shuffling footsteps approaching the door from the inside. It seemed, as the Mole remarked to the Rat, like someone walking in carpet slippers that were too large for him and down-at-heel, which was intelligent of Mole, because that was exactly what it was.

There was the noise of a bolt shot back, and the door opened a few inches, enough to show a long snout and a pair of sleepy blinking eyes.

'Now, the *very* next time this happens,' said a gruff and suspicious voice, 'I shall be exceedingly angry. Who is it *this* time, disturbing people on such a night? Speak up!'

'O, Badger,' cried the Rat, 'let us in, please. It's me, Rat, and my friend Mole, and we've lost our way in the snow.'

'What, Ratty, my dear little man!' exclaimed the Badger, in quite a different voice. 'Come along in, both of you, at once. Why, you must be perished. Well I never! Lost in the snow! And in the Wild Wood too, and at this time of night! But come in with you.'

The two animals tumbled over each other in their eagerness to get inside, and heard the door shut behind them with great joy and relief.

The Badger, who wore a long dressing-gown, and whose slippers were indeed very down-at-heel, carried a flat candlestick in his paw and had probably been on his way to bed when their summons sounded. He looked kindly down on them and patted both their heads. 'This is not the sort of night for small animals to be out,' he said paternally. 'I'm afraid you've been up to some of your pranks again, Ratty. But come along, come into the kitchen. There's a first-rate fire there, and supper and everything.'

He shuffled on in front of them, carrying the light, and they followed him, nudging each other in an anticipating sort of way, down a long, gloomy, and to tell the truth, decidedly shabby passage, into a sort of a central hall, out of which they could dimly see other long tunnel-like passages branching, passages mysterious and without apparent end. But there were doors in the hall as well – stout oaken comfortable-looking doors. One of these the Badger flung open, and at once they found themselves in all the glow and warmth of a large fire-lit kitchen.

The floor was well-worn red brick, and on the wide hearth burnt a fire of logs, between two attractive chimney-corners tucked away in the wall, well out of any suspicion of draught. A couple of high-backed settles, facing each other on either side of the fire, gave further sitting accommodation for the sociably disposed. In the middle of the room stood a long table of plain boards placed on trestles, with benches down each side. At one end of it, where an arm-chair stood pushed back, were spread the remains of the Badger's plain but ample supper. Rows of spotless plates winked from the shelves of the dresser at the far end of the room, and from the rafters overhead hung hams, bundles of dried herbs, nets of onions, and baskets of eggs. The ruddy brick floor smiled up at the smoky ceiling; the oaken settles, shiny with long wear, exchanged cheerful glances with each other; plates on the dresser grinned at pots on the shelf, and the merry firelight flickered and played over everything without distinction.

The kindly Badger thrust them down on a settle to toast themselves at the fire, and bade them remove their wet coats and boots. Then he fetched them dressing-gowns and slippers, and himself bathed the Mole's shin with warm water and mended the cut with sticking-plaster till the whole thing was just as good as new, if not

better. In the embracing light and warmth, warm
and dry at last, with weary legs propped up in
front of them, and a suggestive clink of plates
being arranged on the table behind, it seemed to
the storm-driven animals, now in safe anchor-
age, that the cold and trackless Wild Wood just
left outside was miles and miles away, and all
that they had suffered in it a half-forgotten
dream.

When at last they were thoroughly toasted,
the Badger summoned them to the table, where
he had been busy laying a repast. He sat in his
arm-chair at the head of the table and nodded

gravely at intervals as the animals told their story. The Mole began to feel very friendly towards him.

When supper was really finished at last, they gathered round the glowing embers of the great wood fire and, after they had chatted for a time about things in general, the Badger said heartily, 'Now then! tell us the news from your part of the world. How's old Toad going on?'

'O, from bad to worse,' said the Rat gravely, while the Mole, cocked up on a settle and basking in the firelight, tried to look properly mournful. 'Another smash-up only last week, and a bad one. You see, he will insist on driving himself, and he's hopelessly incapable. If he'd only employ a decent, steady, well-trained animal, pay him good wages, and leave everything to him, he'd get on all right. But no, he's convinced he's a heaven-born driver, and nobody can teach him anything, and all the rest follows.'

'How many has he had?' inquired the Badger gloomily.

'Smashes, or machines?' asked the Rat. 'O, well, after all, it's the same thing – with Toad. This is the seventh. As for the others – you know that coach-house of his? Well, it's piled up – literally piled up to the roof – with fragments of motor-cars, none of them bigger than your hat! That accounts for the other six – so far as they can be accounted for.'

'He's been in hospital three times,' put in the Mole, 'and as for the fines he's had to pay, it's simply awful to think of.'

'Yes, and that's part of the trouble,' continued the Rat. 'Toad's rich, we all know, but he's not a millionaire. And he's a hopelessly bad driver, and quite regardless of law and order. Killed or ruined – it's got to be one of the two things, sooner or later. Badger! we're his friends – oughtn't we to do something?'

The Badger went through a bit of hard thinking. 'Now look here!' he said at last, rather severely, 'of course you know I can't do anything *now*?'

His two friends assented, quite understanding his point. No animal is ever expected to do anything strenuous during the winter. All are sleepy – some actually asleep. All are weather-bound, more or less, and all are resting from arduous days and nights, during which every muscle in them has been severely tested, and every energy kept at full stretch.

'Very well then!' continued the Badger. '*But*, when once the year has really turned, and the nights are shorter, and half-way through them one rouses and feels fidgety and wanting to be up and doing by sunrise, if not before, *then* we'll take Toad seriously in hand. We'll stand no nonsense whatever. We'll bring him back to reason, by force if need be. We'll *make* him be a sensible Toad!'

5

Mr Toad

It was a bright morning in the early part of summer. The Mole and the Water Rat had been up since dawn, very busy on matters connected with boats and the opening of the boating season (painting and varnishing, mending paddles, repairing cushions, hunting for missing boat-hooks, and so on) and were finishing breakfast in their little parlour and eagerly discussing their plans for the day, when a heavy knock sounded at the door.

'Bother!' said the Rat, all over egg. 'See who it is, Mole, like a good chap, since you've finished.'

The Mole went to attend the summons, and the Rat heard him utter a cry of surprise. Then he flung the parlour door open, and announced with much importance, 'Mr Badger!'

This was a wonderful thing, indeed, that the Badger should pay a formal call on them, or indeed on anybody!

The Badger strode heavily into the room and stood looking at the two animals with an expression full of seriousness. The Rat let his egg-spoon fall on the tablecloth and sat open-mouthed.

'The hour has come!' said the Badger at last with great solemnity.

'What hour?' asked the Rat uneasily, glancing at the clock on the mantelpiece.

'*Whose* hour, you should rather say,' replied

the Badger. 'Why, Toad's hour! The hour of Toad! I said I would take him in hand as soon as the winter was well over, and I'm going to take him in hand today!'

'Toad's hour, of course!' cried the Mole delightedly. 'Hooray! I remember now! *We'll* teach him to be a sensible Toad!'

'This very morning,' continued the Badger, taking an arm-chair, 'as I learnt last night from a trustworthy source, another new and exceptionally powerful motor-car will arrive at Toad Hall on approval or return. At this very moment, perhaps, Toad is busily arraying himself in those singularly hideous habiliments so dear to him, which transform him from a (comparatively) good-looking Toad into an Object which throws any decent-minded animal that comes across it into a violent fit. We must be up and doing, ere it is too late. You two animals will accompany me instantly to Toad Hall, and the work of rescue shall be accomplished.'

'Right you are!' cried the Rat, starting up. 'We'll rescue the poor unhappy animal! We'll convert him! He'll be the most converted Toad that ever was before we've done with him!'

They set off up the road on their mission of
mercy, Badger leading the way.

When they reached the carriage-drive of Toad
Hall they found, as the Badger had anticipated,
a shiny new motor-car, of great size, painted a
bright red (Toad's favourite colour), standing in
front of the house. As they neared the door it was
flung open, and Mr Toad, arrayed in goggles,
cap, gaiters, and enormous overcoat, came

swaggering down the steps, drawing on his gauntleted gloves.

'Hullo! Come on, you fellows!' he cried cheerfully on catching sight of them. 'You're just in time to come with me for a jolly – to come for a jolly – for a – er – jolly –'

His hearty accents faltered and fell away as he noticed the stern look on the countenances of his silent friends, and his invitation remained unfinished.

The Badger strode up the steps. 'Take him inside,' he said sternly to his companions. Then, as Toad was hustled through the door, he turned to the chauffeur in charge of the new motor-car.

'I'm afraid you won't be wanted today,' he said. 'Mr Toad has changed his mind. He will not require the car. Please understand that this is final. You needn't wait.' Then he followed the others inside and shut the door.

'Now, then!' he said to the Toad, when the four of them stood together in the hall, 'first of all, take those ridiculous things off!'

'Shan't!' replied Toad, with great spirit. 'What is the meaning of this gross outrage? I demand an instant explanation.'

'Take them off him, then, you two,' ordered the Badger briefly.

They had to lay Toad out on the floor, kicking and calling all sorts of names, before they could get to work properly. Then the Rat sat on him, and the Mole got his motor-clothes off him bit by bit, and they stood him up on his legs again. A good deal of his blustering spirit seemed to have evaporated with the removal of his fine panoply. Now that he was merely Toad, and no longer the Terror of the Highway, he giggled feebly and looked from one to the other appealingly, seeming not quite to understand the situation.

'You knew it must come to this, sooner or later, Toad,' the Badger explained severely. 'You've disregarded all the warnings we've given you, you've gone on squandering the money your father left you, and you're getting us animals a bad name in the district by your furious driving and your smashes and your rows with the police. Now, you're a good fellow in many respects, and I don't want to be too hard on you. I'll make one more effort to bring you to reason. You will come with me into the smoking-room, and there you will hear some facts about yourself, and we'll see whether you come out of that room the same Toad that you went in.'

He took Toad firmly by the arm, led him into the smoking-room, and closed the door behind them.

'*That's* no good!' said the Rat contemptuously. '*Talking* to Toad'll never cure him. He'll *say* anything.'

They made themselves comfortable in arm-chairs and waited patiently. Through the closed door they could just hear the long continuous drone of the Badger's voice, rising and falling in waves of oratory, and presently they noticed that the sermon began to be punctuated at intervals by long-drawn sobs, evidently proceeding from the bosom of Toad, who was a soft-hearted and affectionate fellow, very easily converted – for the time being – to any point of view.

After some three-quarters of an hour the door opened, and the Badger reappeared, solemnly leading by the paw a very limp and dejected Toad. His skin hung baggily about him, his legs wobbled, and his cheeks were furrowed by the tears so plentifully called forth by the Badger's moving discourse.

'Sit down there, Toad,' said the Badger kindly, pointing to a chair. 'My friends,' he went on, 'I am pleased to inform you that Toad has at last seen the error of his ways. He is truly sorry for his misguided conduct in the past, and he has undertaken to give up motor-cars entirely and for ever. I have his solemn promise to that effect.'

'That is very good news,' said the Mole gravely.

'There's only one thing more to be done,' continued the Badger. 'Toad, I want you solemnly to repeat, before your friends here, what you fully admitted to me in the smoking-room just now. First, you are sorry for what you've done, and you see the folly of it all.'

There was a long, long pause. Toad looked desperately this way and that, while the other animals waited in grave silence. At last he spoke.

'No!' he said a little sullenly, but stoutly, 'I'm *not* sorry. And it wasn't folly at all! It was simply glorious!'

'What?' cried the Badger, greatly scandalized. 'You backsliding animal, didn't you tell me just now, in there –'

'O, yes, yes,' said Toad impatiently. 'I'd have said anything in *there*. You're so eloquent, dear Badger, and so moving, and so convincing, and put all your points so frightfully well – you can do what you like with me in *there*, and you know it. But I've been searching my mind since, and going over things in it, and I find that I'm not a bit sorry or repentant really, so it's no earthly good saying I am; now, is it?'

'Then you don't promise,' said the Badger, 'never to touch a motor-car again?'

'Certainly not!' replied Toad emphatically. 'On the contrary, I faithfully promise that the very first motor-car I see, poop-poop! off I go in it!'

'Told you so, didn't I?' observed the Rat to the Mole.

'Very well, then,' said the Badger firmly, rising to his feet. 'Since you won't yield to persuasion, we'll try what force can do. I feared it would come to this all along. You've often asked us three to come and stay with you, Toad, in this handsome house of yours; well, now we're going to. When we've converted you to a proper point of view we may quit, but not before. Take him upstairs, you two, and lock him up in his bed-room, while we arrange matters between our-selves.'

'It's for your own good, Toady, you know,' said the Rat kindly, as Toad, kicking and strug-gling, was hauled up the stairs by his two faithful friends. 'Think what fun we shall all have to-gether, just as we used to, when you've quite got over this – this painful attack of yours!'

'We'll take care of everything for you till you're well, Toad,' said the Mole, 'and we'll see your money isn't wasted, as it has been.'

'No more of those regrettable incidents with the police, Toad,' said the Rat, as they thrust him into his bedroom.

'And no more weeks in hospital, being ordered about by nurses, Toad,' added the Mole, turning the key on him.

They descended the stairs, Toad shouting abuse at them through the keyhole, and the three friends then met in conference on the situation.

'It's going to be a tedious business,' said the Badger, sighing. 'I've never seen Toad so determined. However, we will see it out. He must never be left an instant unguarded. We shall have to take it in turns to be with him, till the poison has worked itself out of his system.'

They arranged watches accordingly. Each animal took it in turns to sleep in Toad's room at night, and they divided the day up between them. But Toad's interest in other matters did not seem to revive, and he grew apparently languid and depressed.

One fine morning the Rat, whose turn it was to go on duty, went upstairs to relieve Badger, whom he found fidgeting to be off and stretch his legs in a long ramble round his wood and down his earths and burrows. 'Toad's still in bed,' he told the Rat, outside the door. 'Can't get much out of him, except, "O, leave him alone, he wants nothing, perhaps he'll be better presently, it may pass off in time, don't be unduly anxious," and so on. Now, you look out, Rat! When Toad's quiet and submissive, and playing at being the hero of a Sunday-school prize, then he's at his artfullest. There's sure to be something up. I know him. Well, now I must be off.'

'How are you today, old chap?' inquired the Rat cheerfully, as he approached Toad's bedside.

He had to wait some minutes for an answer. At last a feeble voice replied, 'Thank you so much, dear Ratty! So good of you to inquire! But first tell me how you are yourself, and the excellent Mole?'

'O, *we're* all right,' replied the Rat. 'Mole,' he added incautiously, 'is going out for a run round with Badger. They'll be out till luncheon-time, so you and I will spend a pleasant morning together, and I'll do my best to amuse you. Now jump up, there's a good fellow, and don't lie moping there on a fine morning like this!'

'Dear, kind Rat,' murmured Toad, 'how little you realize my condition, and how very far I am from "jumping up" now – if ever! But do not trouble about me. I hate being a burden to my friends, and I do not expect to be one much longer. Indeed, I almost hope not.'

'Well, I hope not, too,' said the Rat heartily. 'You've been a fine bother to us all this time, and I'm glad to hear it's going to stop. And in weather like this, and the boating season just beginning! It's too bad of you, Toad! It isn't the trouble we mind, but you're making us miss such an awful lot.'

'I'm afraid it *is* the trouble you mind, though,' replied the Toad languidly. 'I can quite understand it. It's natural enough. You're tired of bothering about me. I mustn't ask you to do anything further. I'm a nuisance, I know.'

'You are, indeed,' said the Rat. 'But I tell you, I'd take any trouble on earth for you, if only you'd be a sensible animal.'

'If I thought that, Ratty,' murmured Toad, more feebly than ever, 'then I would beg you – for the last time, probably – to step round to the village as quickly as possible – even now it may be too late – and fetch the doctor. But don't you bother. It's only a trouble, and perhaps we may as well let things take their course.'

'Why, what do you want a doctor for?' inquired the Rat, coming closer and examining him. He certainly lay very still and flat, and his voice was weaker and his manner much changed.

'Surely you have noticed of late –' murmured Toad. 'But no – why should you? Noticing things is only a trouble. Tomorrow, indeed, you may be saying to yourself, "O, if only I had noticed sooner! If only I had done something!" But no, it's a trouble. Never mind – forget that I asked.'

'Look here, old man,' said the Rat, beginning to get rather alarmed, 'of course I'll fetch a doctor to you, if you really think you want him. But you can hardly be bad enough for that yet. Let's talk about something else.'

'I fear, dear friend,' said Toad, with a sad smile, 'that "talk" can do little in a case like this – or doctors either, for that matter. Still, one must grasp at the slightest straw. And, by the way – while you are about it – I *hate* to give you additional trouble, but I happen to remember that you will pass the door – would you mind at the same time asking the lawyer to step up?'

'A lawyer! O, he must be really bad!' the affrighted Rat said to himself, as he hurried from the room, not forgetting, however, to lock the door carefully behind him.

Outside, he stopped to consider. The other two were far away, and he had no one to consult.

'It's best to be on the safe side,' he said, on reflection. 'I've known Toad fancy himself frightfully bad before, without the slightest reason, but I've never heard him ask for a lawyer! If there's nothing really the matter, the doctor will tell him he's an old ass and cheer him up, and that will be something gained. I'd better humour him and go. It won't take very long.' So he ran off to the village on his errand of mercy.

The Toad, who had hopped lightly out of bed as soon as he heard the key turned in the lock, watched him eagerly from the window till he disappeared down the carriage-drive. Then, laughing heartily, he dressed as quickly as possible in the smartest suit he could lay hands on at the moment, filled his pockets with cash which

he took from a small drawer in the dressing-
table, and next, knotting the sheets from his bed
together and tying one end of the improvised
rope round the central mullion of the handsome
Tudor window which formed such a feature of
his bedroom, he scrambled out, slid lightly to the
ground, and, taking the opposite direction to
the Rat, marched off lightheartedly, whistling a
merry tune.

It was a gloomy luncheon for Rat when the
Badger and the Mole at length returned, and he
had to face them at table with his pitiful and

unconvincing story. Even the Mole, though he took his friend's side as far as possible, could not help saying, 'You've been a bit of a duffer this time, Ratty! Toad, too, of all animals!'

Meanwhile, Toad, gay and irresponsible, was walking briskly along the high road, some miles from home.

'Smart piece of work that!' he remarked to himself, chuckling. 'Brain against brute force – and brain came out on the top – as it's bound to do. Poor old Ratty! My! won't he catch it when the Badger gets back! A worthy fellow, Ratty, with many good qualities, but very little intelligence and absolutely no education. I must take him in hand some day, and see if I can make something of him.'

Filled full of conceited thoughts such as these he strode along, his head in the air, till he reached a little town, where the sign of 'The Red Lion', swinging across the road half-way down the main street, reminded him that he had not breakfasted that day, and that he was exceedingly hungry after his long walk. He marched into the inn, ordered the best luncheon that could be provided at so short a notice, and sat down to eat it in the coffee-room.

He was about half-way through his meal when an only too familiar sound, approaching down the street, made him start and fall a-trembling all over. The poop-poop! drew nearer and nearer, the car could be heard to turn into the inn-yard and come to a stop, and Toad had to hold on to the leg of the table to conceal his overmastering emotion. Presently the party entered the coffee-room, hungry, talkative and gay, voluble on their experiences of the morning and the merits of the chariot that had brought them along so well. Toad listened eagerly, all ears, for a time. At last he could stand it no longer. He slipped out of the room quietly, paid his bill at the bar, and as soon as he got outside sauntered round quietly to the inn-yard. 'There cannot be any harm,' he said to himself, 'in my only just *looking* at it!'

The car stood in the middle of the yard, quite unattended. Toad walked slowly round it, inspecting, criticizing, musing deeply.

'I wonder,' he said to himself presently, 'I wonder if this sort of car *starts* easily?'

Next moment, hardly knowing how it came about, he found he had hold of the handle and was turning it. As the familiar sound broke forth, the old passion seized on Toad and completely mastered him, body and soul. As if in a dream he found himself, somehow, seated in the driver's seat; as if in a dream, he pulled the lever and swung the car round the yard and out through the archway. He increased his pace and, as the car devoured the street and leapt forth on the high road through the open country, he was only conscious that he was Toad once more, Toad at his best and highest, Toad the terror,

Toad the traffic-queller. He chanted as he flew, and the car responded with sonorous drone; the miles were eaten up under him as he sped he knew not whither, fulfilling his instincts, living his hour, reckless of what might come to him.

6

The Dungeon

The rusty key creaked in the lock, the great door clanged behind him, and Toad was a helpless prisoner in the remotest dungeon of the best-guarded keep of the stoutest castle in all the length and breadth of Merry England.

When Toad found himself immured in this dank and noisome dungeon, and knew that all the grim darkness of a medieval fortress lay between him and the outer world of sunshine and well-metalled high roads where he had lately been so happy, he flung himself at full length on the floor, and shed bitter tears. 'This is the end of everything' (he said), 'at least it is the end of the career of Toad, which is the same thing; the popular and handsome Toad, the rich and hospitable Toad, the Toad so free and careless and debonair! How can I hope to be ever set at large again' (he said), 'who have been imprisoned so justly for stealing so handsome a motor-car! Stupid animal that I was' (he said), 'now I must languish in this dungeon, till people who were proud to say they knew me, have forgotten the very name of Toad!' With lamentations such as these he passed his days and nights for several weeks, refusing his meals or intermediate light refreshments.

Now the gaoler had a daughter, a pleasant wench and good-hearted, who assisted her father in the lighter duties of his post. She was particularly fond of animals, and, besides her canary, she kept several piebald mice and a restless revolving squirrel. This kind-hearted girl, pitying the misery of Toad, said to her father one day, 'Father! I can't bear to see that poor beast so unhappy, and getting so thin! You let me have the managing of him. You know how fond of animals I am. I'll make him eat from my hand, and sit up, and do all sorts of things.'

Her father replied that she could do what she liked with him. He was tired of Toad, and his sulks and his airs. So that day she went on her errand of mercy, and knocked at the door of Toad's cell.

'Now, cheer up, Toad,' she said coaxingly, on entering, 'and sit up and dry your eyes and be a sensible animal. And do try and eat a bit of dinner. See, I've brought you some of mine, hot from the oven!'

It was bubble-and-squeak, between two plates, and its fragrance filled the narrow cell. The penetrating smell of cabbage reached the nose of Toad as he lay prostrate on the floor, and gave him the idea for a moment that perhaps life was not such a blank and desperate thing as he had imagined. But still he wailed, and kicked with his legs, and refused to be comforted. So the wise girl retired for the time, but, of course, a good deal of the smell of hot cabbage remained behind, as it will do, and Toad, between his sobs, sniffed and reflected, and gradually began to think of his friends, and how they would surely be able to do something; of his own great cleverness and resource, and all that he was capable of if he only gave his great mind to it.

When the gaoler's daughter returned, some hours later, she carried a tray, with a cup of fragrant tea steaming on it; and a plate piled up with very hot buttered toast, cut thick, very brown on both sides, with the butter running through the holes in it in great golden drops, like honey from the honeycomb. The smell of that buttered toast simply talked to Toad, and with no uncertain voice; talked of warm kitchens, of breakfasts on bright frosty mornings, of cosy parlour firesides on winter evenings, when one's ramble was over and slippered feet were propped on the fender; of the purring of contented cats, and the twitter of sleepy canaries. Toad sat up on end once more, dried his eyes, sipped his tea and munched his toast, and soon began talking freely about himself, and the house he lived in, and his doings there, and how important he was, and what a lot his friends thought of him.

When the girl said good night, having filled his water-jug and shaken up his straw for him, Toad was very much the same sanguine, self-satisfied animal that he had been of old. He sang a little song or two, of the sort he used to sing at his dinner-parties, curled himself up in the straw, and had an excellent night's rest and the pleasantest of dreams.

They had many interesting talks together, after that, as the dreary days went on; and the gaoler's daughter grew very sorry for Toad, and thought it a great shame that a poor little animal should be locked up in prison for what seemed to her a very trivial offence.

One morning she was very thoughtful and did not seem to Toad to be paying proper attention to his witty sayings and sparkling comments.

'Toad,' she said presently, 'just listen, please. I have an aunt who is a washerwoman.'

'There, there,' said Toad graciously and affably, 'never mind, think no more about it. *I* have several aunts who *ought* to be washer-women.'

'Do be quiet a minute, Toad,' said the girl. 'You talk too much, that's your chief fault, and I'm trying to think, and you hurt my head. As I said, I have an aunt who is a washerwoman. She does the washing for all the prisoners in this castle. Now, this is what occurs to me: you're very rich – at least you're always telling me so – and she's very poor. A few pounds wouldn't make any difference to you, and it would mean a lot to her. Now, I think if she were properly approached, you could come to some arrange-ment by which she would let you have her dress and bonnet and so on, and you could escape from the castle as the official washerwoman. You're very alike in many respects – particularly about the figure.'

'We're *not*,' said the Toad in a huff. 'I have a very elegant figure – for what I am.'

'So has my aunt,' replied the girl, 'for what *she* is. But have it your own way. You horrid, proud, ungrateful animal, when I'm sorry for you, and trying to help you!'

'Yes, yes, that's all right; thank you very much indeed,' said the Toad hurriedly. 'But look here! you wouldn't surely have Mr Toad, of Toad Hall, going about the country disguised as a washerwoman!'

'Then you can stop here as a Toad,' replied the girl with much spirit. 'I suppose you want to go off in a coach-and-four!'

Honest Toad was always ready to admit himself in the wrong. 'You are a good, kind, clever girl,' he said, 'and I am indeed a proud and a stupid toad. Introduce me to your worthy aunt, if you will be so kind, and I have no doubt that the excellent lady and I will be able to arrange terms satisfactory to both parties.'

Next evening the girl ushered her aunt into Toad's cell, bearing his week's washing pinned up in a towel. The old lady had been prepared beforehand for the interview, and the sight of certain golden sovereigns that Toad had thoughtfully placed on the table in full view practically completed the matter and left little further to discuss. In return for his cash, Toad received a cotton print gown, an apron, a shawl, and a rusty black bonnet; the only stipulation the old lady made being that she should be gagged and bound and dumped down in a corner. By this not very convincing artifice, she explained, she hoped to retain her situation, in spite of the suspicious appearance of things.

Toad was delighted with the suggestion. It would enable him to leave the prison in some style, and with his reputation for being a desperate and dangerous fellow untarnished; and he readily helped the gaoler's daughter to make her aunt appear as much as possible the victim of circumstances over which she had no control.

'Now it's your turn, Toad,' said the girl. 'Take off that coat and waistcoat of yours; you're fat enough as it is.'

Shaking with laughter, she proceeded to 'hook-and-eye' him into the cotton print gown, arranged the shawl with a professional fold, and tied the strings of the rusty bonnet under his chin.

'You're the very image of her,' she giggled, 'only I'm sure you never looked half so respectable in all your life before. Now, good-bye, Toad, and good luck. Go straight down the way you came up; and if anyone says anything to you, as they probably will, being but men, you can chaff back a bit, of course, but remember you're a widow woman, quite alone in the world, with a character to lose.'

With a quaking heart, but as firm a footstep as he could command, Toad set forth cautiously on what seemed to be a most hare-brained and

hazardous undertaking; but he was soon agree-
ably surprised to find how easy everything was
made for him. The washerwoman's squat figure
in its familiar cotton print seemed a passport for
every barred door and grim gateway; even when
he hesitated, uncertain as to the right turning to
take, he found himself helped out of his difficulty
by the warder at the next gate, anxious to be off
to his tea, summoning him to come along sharp
and not keep him waiting there all night.

It seemed hours before he crossed the last
courtyard, but at last he heard the wicket-gate in
the great outer door click behind him, felt the
fresh air of the outer world upon his anxious
brow, and knew that he was free!

7

The Engine

As Toad walked quickly away his attention was caught by some red and green lights a little way off, to one side of the town, and the sound of the puffing and snorting of engines and the banging of shunted trucks fell on his ear. 'Aha!' he thought, 'this is a piece of luck! A railway-station is the thing I want most in the whole world at this moment!'

He made his way to the station accordingly, consulted a time-table, and found that a train, bound more or less in the direction of his home, was due to start in half an hour. 'More luck!' said Toad, his spirits rising rapidly, and went off to the booking-office to buy his ticket.

He gave the name of the station, and mechanically put his fingers, in search of the necessary money, where his waistcoat pocket should have been, but he found – not only no money, but no pocket to hold it, and no waistcoat to hold the pocket!

To his horror he recollected that he had left both coat and waistcoat behind him in his cell, and with them his pocket-book, money, keys, watch, matches, pencil-case – all that makes life worth living.

Baffled and full of despair, Toad wandered blindly down the platform where the train was standing and tears trickled down each side of his nose.

'Hullo, mother!' said the engine-driver, a burly man with an oil-can in one hand and a lump of cotton-waste in the other. 'What's the trouble? You don't look particularly cheerful.'

'O, sir!' said Toad, crying afresh, 'I am a poor unhappy washerwoman, and I've lost all my money, and can't pay for a ticket, and I *must* get home tonight somehow, and whatever I am to do I don't know. O dear, O dear!'

'That's a bad business, indeed,' said the engine-driver reflectively. 'Lost your money – and can't get home – and got some kids, too, waiting for you, I dare say?'

'Any amount of 'em,' sobbed Toad. 'And they'll be hungry – and playing with matches – and upsetting lamps, the little innocents! – and quarrelling, and going on generally. O dear, O dear!'

'Well, I'll tell you what I'll do,' said the good engine-driver. 'You're a washerwoman to your trade, says you. Very well, that's that. And I'm an engine-driver, as you well may see, and there's no denying it's terribly dirty work. Uses up a power of shirts, it does, till my missus is fair tired of washing of 'em. If you'll wash a few shirts for me when you get home, and send 'em along, I'll give you a ride on my engine. It's against the Company's regulations, but we're not so very particular in these out-of-the-way parts.'

The Toad's misery turned into rapture as he eagerly scrambled up into the cab of the engine. Of course, he had never washed a shirt in his life, and couldn't if he tried and, anyhow, he wasn't going to begin, but he thought: 'When I get safely home to Toad Hall, and have money again, and pockets to put it in, I will send the engine-driver enough to pay for quite a quantity of washing, and that will be the same thing, or better.'

The guard waved his welcome flag, the engine-driver whistled in cheerful response, and the train moved out of the station. As the speed increased, and the Toad could see on either side of him real fields, and trees, and hedges, and cows, and horses, all flying past him, and as he thought how every minute was bringing him nearer to Toad Hall, and a soft bed to sleep in, and good things to eat, and praise and admiration at the recital of his adventures and his surpassing cleverness, he began to skip up and down and shout and sing snatches of song, to the great astonishment of the engine-driver, who had come across washerwomen before, at long intervals, but never one at all like this.

They had covered many and many a mile, and Toad was already considering what he would have for supper as soon as he got home, when he noticed that the engine-driver, with a puzzled expression on his face, was leaning over the side of the engine and listening hard. Then he saw him climb on to the coals and gaze out over the top of the train, then he returned and said to Toad: 'It's very strange, we're the last train running in this direction tonight, yet I could be sworn that I heard another following us!'

Toad ceased his frivolous antics at once. He became grave and depressed, and a dull pain in the lower part of his spine, communicating itself to his legs, made him want to sit down and try desperately not to think of all the possibilities.

By this time the moon was shining brightly, and the engine-driver, steadying himself on the coal, could command a view of the line behind them for a long distance.

Presently he called out, 'I can see it clearly now! It is an engine, on our rails, coming along at a great pace! It looks as if we were being pursued!'

The miserable Toad, crouching in the coal-dust, tried hard to think of something to do, with dismal want of success.

'They are gaining on us fast!' cried the engine-driver. 'And the engine is crowded with the queerest lot of people, all waving, and all shouting the same thing – "Stop, stop, stop!"'

Then Toad fell on his knees among the coals and, raising his clasped paws in supplication, cried, 'Save me, only save me, dear kind Mr Engine-driver, and I will confess everything! I am not the simple washerwoman I seem to be! I have no children waiting for me, innocent or otherwise! I am a toad – the well-known and popular Mr Toad, a landed proprietor. I have just escaped, by my great daring and cleverness, from a loathsome dungeon into which my enemies had flung me, and if those fellows on that engine recapture me, it will be chains and bread-and-water and straw and misery once more for poor, unhappy, innocent Toad!'

The engine-driver looked down upon him very sternly, and said, 'Now tell the truth, what were you put in prison for?'

'It was nothing very much,' said poor Toad, colouring deeply. 'I only borrowed a motor-car while the owners were at lunch; they had no need of it at the time. I didn't mean to steal it, really, but people – especially magistrates – take such harsh views of thoughtless and high-spirited actions.'

The engine-driver looked very grave and said, 'I fear that you have been indeed a wicked toad, and by rights I ought to give you up to offended justice. But the sight of an animal in tears always makes me feel queer and soft-hearted. So cheer up, Toad! I'll do my best, and we may beat them yet!'

They piled on more coals, shovelling furiously. The furnace roared, the sparks flew, the

engine leapt and swung, but still their pursuers
slowly gained. The engine-driver, with a sigh,
wiped his brow with a handful of cotton-waste,
and said, 'I'm afraid it's no good, Toad. You see,
they are running light, and they have the better
engine. There's just one thing left for us to do,
and it's your only chance, so attend very carefully to what I tell you. A short way ahead of us
is a long tunnel, and on the other side of that the
line passes through a thick wood. Now, I will put
on all the speed I can while we are running
through the tunnel, but the other fellows will
slow down a bit, naturally, for fear of an
accident. When we are through, I will shut off
steam and put on brakes as hard as I can, and the
moment it's safe to do so you must jump and hide
in the wood, before they get through the tunnel

and see you. Then I will go full speed ahead again, and they can chase *me* if they like, for as long as they like, and as far as they like. Now mind and be ready to jump when I tell you!'

They piled on more coals, and the train shot into the tunnel, and the engine rushed and roared and rattled, till at last they shot out at the other end into fresh air and the peaceful moonlight, and saw the wood lying dark and helpful upon either side of the line. The driver shut off steam and put on brakes, the Toad got down on the step, and as the train slowed down to almost a walking pace he heard the driver call out, 'Now, jump!'

Toad jumped, rolled down a short embankment, picked himself up unhurt, scrambled into the wood and hid in a hollow tree, where, with branches and dead leaves, he made himself as comfortable a bed as he could, and slept soundly till the morning.

8

The Barge

The front door of the hollow tree faced eastwards, so Toad was called at an early hour, partly by the bright sunlight streaming in on him, partly by the exceeding coldness of his toes. He shook himself and combed the dry leaves out of his hair with his fingers, and, his toilet complete, marched forth into the comfortable morning sun, cold but confident, hungry but hopeful.

Presently he came to a canal, and round a bend in the canal came plodding a solitary horse. Toad let the horse pass and stood waiting for the barge it was pulling.

With a pleasant swirl of quiet water at its blunt bow the barge slid up alongside of him, its gaily painted gunwale level with the towing-path, its sole occupant a big stout woman wearing a linen sun-bonnet, one brawny arm laid along the tiller.

'A nice morning, ma'am!' she remarked to Toad, as she drew up level with him.

'I dare say it is, ma'am!' responded Toad politely, as he walked along the tow-path abreast of her. 'I dare say it *is* a nice morning to them that's not in sore trouble, like what I am. Here's my married daughter, she sends off to me post-haste to come to her at once, so off I comes, not knowing what may be happening or going to happen, but fearing the worst, as you will understand, ma'am, if you're a mother, too. And I've left my business to look after itself – I'm in the washing and laundering line, you must know, ma'am – and I've left my young children to look after themselves, and a more mischievous and troublesome set of young imps doesn't exist, ma'am; and I've lost all my money, and lost my way, and as for what may be happening to my married daughter, why, I don't like to think of it, ma'am!'

'Where might your married daughter be living, ma'am?' asked the barge-woman.

'She lives near to the river, ma'am,' replied Toad. 'Close to a fine house called Toad Hall, that's somewheres hereabouts in these parts. Perhaps you may have heard of it.'

'Toad Hall? Why, I'm going that way myself,' replied the barge-woman. 'This canal joins the river some miles further on, a little above Toad Hall, and then it's an easy walk. You come along in the barge with me, and I'll give you a lift.'

She steered the barge close to the bank, and Toad, with many humble and grateful acknowledgements, stepped lightly on board and sat down with great satisfaction. 'Toad's luck again!' thought he. 'I always come out on top!'

'So you're in the washing business, ma'am?' said the barge-woman politely, as they glided along. 'And a very good business you've got too, I dare say, if I'm not making too free in saying so.'

'Finest business in the whole county,' said Toad airily. 'All the gentry come to me — wouldn't go to anyone else if they were paid, they know me so well. You see, I understand my work thoroughly, and attend to it all myself. Washing, ironing, clear-starching, making up gents' fine shirts for evening wear – everything's done under my own eye!'

'But surely you don't *do* all that work yourself, ma'am?' asked the barge-woman respectfully.

'O, I have girls,' said Toad lightly: 'twenty girls or thereabouts, always at work. But you know what *girls* are, ma'am! Nasty little hussies, that's what *I* call 'em!'

'So do I, too,' said the barge-woman with great heartiness. 'But I dare say you set yours to rights, the idle trollops! And are you *very* fond of washing?'

'I love it,' said Toad. 'I simply dote on it. Never so happy as when I've got both arms in the wash-tub. But, then, it comes so easy to me! No trouble at all! A real pleasure, I assure you, ma'am!'

'What a bit of luck, meeting you!' observed the barge-woman thoughtfully. 'A regular piece of good fortune for both of us!'

'Why, what do you mean?' asked Toad nervously.

'Well, look at me, now,' replied the barge-woman. '*I* like washing, too, just the same as you do, and for that matter, whether I like it or not I have got to do all my own, naturally, moving about as I do. Now my husband, he's such a fellow for shirking his work and leaving the barge to me, that never a moment do I get for seeing to my own affairs. By rights he ought to be here now, either steering or attending to the horse, though luckily the horse has sense enough to attend to himself. Instead of which, he's gone off with the dog, to see if they can't pick up a rabbit for dinner somewhere. Says he'll catch me up at the next lock. But meantime, how am I to get on with my washing?'

'O, never mind about the washing,' said Toad, not liking the subject. 'Try and fix your mind on that rabbit. A nice fat young rabbit, I'll be bound. Got any onions?'

'I can't fix my mind on anything but my washing,' said the barge-woman, 'and I wonder you can be talking of rabbits, with such a joyful prospect before you. There's a heap of things of mine that you'll find in a corner of the cabin. If you'll just take one or two of the most necessary sort – I won't venture to describe them to a lady like you, but you'll recognize 'em at a glance – and put them through the wash-tub as we go along, why, it'll be a pleasure to you, as you rightly say, and a real help to me. You'll find a tub handy, and soap, and a kettle on the stove, and a bucket to haul up water from the canal with. Then I shall know you're enjoying your-self, instead of sitting here idle, looking at the scenery and yawning your head off.'

'Here, you let me steer!' said Toad, now thoroughly frightened, 'and then you can get on with your washing your own way. I might spoil your things, or not do 'em as you like. I'm more used to gentlemen's things myself. It's my special line.'

'Let you steer?' replied the barge-woman, laughing. 'It takes some practice to steer a barge properly. Besides, it's dull work, and I want you to be happy. No, you shall do the washing you are so fond of, and I'll stick to the steering that I understand. Don't try and deprive me of the pleasure of giving you a treat!'

Toad was fairly cornered. He looked for escape this way and that, saw that he was too far from the bank for a flying leap, and sullenly resigned himself to his fate. 'If it comes to that,' he thought in desperation, 'I suppose any fool can *wash*!'

He fetched tub, soap, and other necessaries from the cabin, selected a few garments at random, tried to recollect what he had seen in casual glances through laundry windows, and set to.

A long half-hour passed, and every minute of it saw Toad getting crosser and crosser. He tried coaxing, he tried slapping, he tried punching. Nothing that he could do to the things seemed to please them or do them any good. Once or twice he looked nervously over his shoulder at the barge-woman, but she appeared to be gazing out in front of her, absorbed in her steering. His back ached badly, and he noticed with dismay

that his paws were beginning to get all crinkly.
Now Toad was very proud of his paws. He
muttered under his breath words that should
never pass the lips of either washerwomen or
Toads and lost the soap, for the fiftieth time.

A burst of laughter made him straighten himself and look round. The barge-woman was
leaning back and laughing unrestrainedly, till the
tears ran down her cheeks.

'I've been watching you all the time,' she
gasped. 'I thought you must be a humbug all
along, from the conceited way you talked. Pretty
washerwoman you are! Never washed so much
as a dish-clout in your life, I'll lay!'

Toad's temper, which had been simmering viciously for some time, now fairly boiled over, and he lost all control of himself.

'You common, low, *fat* barge-woman!' he shouted, 'don't you dare to talk to your betters like that! Washerwoman indeed! I would have you to know that I am a Toad, a very well-known, respected, distinguished Toad! I may be under a bit of a cloud at present, but I will *not* be laughed at by a barge-woman!'

The woman moved nearer to him and peered under his bonnet keenly and closely. 'Why, so you are!' she cried. 'Well, I never! A horrid, nasty, crawly Toad! And in my nice clean barge, too! Now that is a thing that I will *not* have.'

She relinquished the tiller for a moment. One big mottled arm shot out and caught Toad by a fore-leg, while the other gripped him fast by a hind-leg. Then the world turned suddenly upside down, the barge seemed to flit lightly across the sky, the wind whistled in his ears, and Toad found himself flying through the air.

The water, when he eventually reached it with a loud splash, proved quite cold enough for his taste. He rose to the surface spluttering, and when he had wiped the duckweed out of his eyes the first thing he saw was the fat barge-woman looking back at him over the stern of the retreating barge and laughing, and he vowed, as he coughed and choked, to be even with her.

9

Be Careful, Washerwoman!

Toad struck out for the shore, but the cotton gown greatly impeded his efforts, and when at length he touched land he found it hard to climb up the steep bank unassisted. He had to take a minute or two's rest to recover his breath, then, gathering his wet skirts well over his arms, he started to run after the barge as fast as his legs would carry him.

The barge-woman was still laughing when he drew up level with her. 'Put yourself through your mangle, washerwoman,' she called out, 'and iron your face and crimp it, and you'll pass for quite a decent-looking Toad!'

Toad never paused to reply. He saw what he wanted ahead of him. Running swiftly on he overtook the horse, unfastened the tow-rope and cast off, jumped lightly on the horse's back, and urged it to a gallop by kicking it vigorously in the sides. He steered for the open country, abandoning the tow-path, and swinging his steed down a rutty lane.

The barge-horse was not capable of any very sustained effort, and its gallop soon subsided into a trot, and its trot into an easy walk; but Toad was quite contented with this, knowing that he, at any rate, was moving, and the barge was not. He had quite recovered his temper, now that he had done something he thought really clever, and he was satisfied to jog along quietly in the sun, taking advantage of any byways and bridle-paths, and trying to forget how very long it was since he had had a square meal, till the canal had been left very far behind him.

He had travelled some miles, his horse and he, and he was feeling drowsy in the hot sunshine, when the horse stopped, lowered his head, and began to nibble the grass, and Toad, waking up, just saved himself from falling off by an effort. He looked about him and found he was on a wide common, dotted with patches of gorse and bramble as far as he could see. Near him stood

a dingy gipsy caravan, and beside it a man was
sitting on a bucket turned upside down, very
busy smoking and staring into the wide world.
A fire of sticks was burning near by, and over the
fire hung an iron pot, and out of that pot came
forth bubblings and gurglings, and a vague suggestive steaminess. Also smells – warm, rich, and
varied smells. So there Toad sat, and sniffed and
sniffed, and looked at the gipsy; and the gipsy sat
and smoked, and looked at him.

Presently the gipsy took his pipe out of his
mouth and remarked in a careless way, 'Want to
sell that there horse of yours?'

Toad was completely taken aback, but the
gipsy's suggestion seemed to smooth the way

towards the two things he wanted so badly – ready money and a solid breakfast.

'What?' he said, 'me sell this beautiful young horse of mine? O no, it's out of the question. Who's going to take the washing home to my customers every week? Besides, I'm too fond of him, and he simply dotes on me.'

'Try and love a donkey,' suggested the gipsy. 'Some people do.'

'You don't seem to see,' continued Toad, 'that this fine horse of mine is a cut above you altogether. He's a blood horse, he is, partly; not the part you see, of course – another part. No, it's not to be thought of for a moment. All the same, how much might you be disposed to offer me for this beautiful young horse of mine?'

The gipsy looked the horse over, and then he looked Toad over with equal care, and looked at the horse again. 'Shillin' a leg,' he said briefly.

'A shilling a leg?' cried Toad. 'If you please, I must take a little time to work that out, and see just what it comes to.'

He climbed down off his horse, and left it to graze, and sat down by the gipsy, and did sums on his fingers, and at last he said, 'A shilling a leg? Why, that comes to exactly four shillings, and no more. O no, I could not think of accepting four shillings for this beautiful young horse of mine.'

'Well,' said the gipsy, 'I'll tell you what I will do. I'll make it five shillings, and that's three-and-sixpence more than the animal's worth. And that's my last word.'

Then Toad sat and pondered long and deeply. At last he said firmly, 'Look here, gipsy! I tell you what we will do, and this is *my* last word. You shall hand me over six shillings and sixpence, cash down; and further, in addition thereto, you shall give me as much breakfast as I can possibly eat, at one sitting of course, out of that iron pot of yours that keeps sending forth such delicious and exciting smells. In return, I will make over to you my spirited young horse, with all the beautiful harness and trappings that are on him, freely thrown in. If that's not good enough for you, say so, and I'll be getting on. I know a man near here who's wanted this horse of mine for years.'

The gipsy grumbled frightfully, but in the end he lugged a dirty canvas bag out of the depths of his trouser-pocket, and counted out six shillings and sixpence into Toad's paw. Then he disappeared into the caravan for an instant, and returned with a large iron plate and a knife, fork, and spoon. He tilted up the pot, and a glorious stream of hot rich stew gurgled into the plate. It was, indeed, the most beautiful stew in the world, being made of partridges, and pheasants, and chickens, and hares, and rabbits, and pea-hens, and guinea-fowls, and one or two other things. Toad took the plate on his lap, almost crying, and stuffed, and stuffed, and stuffed, and stuffed, and kept asking for more, and the gipsy never grudged it him. He thought that he had never eaten so good a breakfast in all his life.

When Toad had taken as much stew on board as he thought he could possibly hold, he got up and said good-bye to the gipsy, and took an affectionate farewell of the horse. The gipsy gave him directions which way to go, and he set forth on his travels again in the best possible spirits. He was, indeed, a very different Toad from the animal of an hour ago. The sun was shining brightly, his wet clothes were quite dry again, he had money in his pockets once more, he was nearing home and friends and safety, and, most and best of all, he had had a substantial meal, hot and nourishing, and felt big, and strong, and careless, and self-confident.

As he tramped along gaily, he thought of his adventures and escapes, and how when things seemed at their worst he had always managed to find a way out, and his pride and conceit began to swell within him. 'Ho, ho!' he said to himself as he marched along with his chin in the air, 'what a clever Toad I am! There is surely no animal equal to me for cleverness in the whole world! My enemies shut me up in prison, encircled by sentries, watched night and day by warders; I walk out through them all, by sheer ability coupled with courage. I am, unfortunately, thrown into a canal by a woman, fat of body and very evil-minded. What of it! I swim ashore, I seize her horse, I ride off in triumph, and I sell the horse for a whole pocketful of money and an excellent breakfast! Ho, ho! I am the Toad, the handsome, the popular, the successful Toad!' He got so puffed up with conceit that he made up a song in praise of himself, and sang it at the top of his voice. It was perhaps the most conceited song that any animal ever composed:

> The world has held great Heroes,
>   As history-books have showed;
> But never a name to go down to fame
>   Compared with that of Toad!
>
> The clever men at Oxford
>   Know all that there is to be knowed;
> But they none of them know one half as much
>   As intelligent Mr Toad!

He sang as he walked, and he walked as he sang, and got more inflated every minute. But his pride was shortly to have a severe fall.

After some miles of country lanes he reached the high road, and as he turned into it and glanced along its white length, he saw approaching him a speck that turned into a dot and then into a blob, and then into something very familiar; and a double 'poop-poop!' of warning fell on his delighted ear.

'This is something like!' said the excited Toad. 'This is real life again, this is once more the great world from which I have been missed so long! I will hail them, my brothers of the wheel, and they will give me a lift, of course, and then I will talk to them some more, and, perhaps, with luck, it may even end in my driving up to Toad Hall in a motor-car!'

He stepped confidently out into the road to hail the motor-car, which came along at an easy pace, slowing down as it neared the lane, when suddenly he became very pale, his heart turned to water, his knees shook and yielded under him, and he doubled up and collapsed with a sickening pain in his interior. And well he might, for the approaching car was the very one he had stolen out of the yard of the Red Lion Hotel on that fatal day when all his troubles began! And the people in it were the very same people he had sat and watched at luncheon in the coffee-room!

He sank down in a shabby, miserable heap in the road, murmuring to himself in his despair, 'It's all up! It's all over now! Chains and policemen again! Prison again! Dry bread and water again! O, what a fool I have been!'

The terrible motor-car drew slowly nearer and nearer, till at last he heard it stop just short of him. Two gentlemen got out and walked round the trembling heap of crumpled misery lying in the road, and one of them said, 'O dear! this is very sad! Here is a poor old thing – a washerwoman apparently – who has fainted in the road! Perhaps she is overcome by the heat, poor creature, or possibly she has not had any food today. Let us lift her into the car and take her to the nearest village, where doubtless she has friends.'

They tenderly lifted Toad into the motor-car and propped him up with soft cushions, and proceeded on their way.

When Toad heard them talk in so kind and sympathetic a manner, he knew that he was not recognized, his courage began to revive, and he cautiously opened first one eye and then the other.

'Look!' said one of the gentlemen, 'she is better already. The fresh air is doing her good. How do you feel now, ma'am?'

'Thank you kindly, sir,' said Toad in a feeble voice, 'I'm feeling a great deal better!'

'That's right,' said the gentleman. 'Now keep quite still, and, above all, don't try to talk.'

'I won't,' said Toad. 'I was only thinking, if I might sit on the front seat there, beside the driver, where I could get the fresh air full in my face, I should soon be all right again.'

'What a very sensible woman!' said the gentleman. 'Of course you shall.' So they carefully helped Toad into the front seat beside the driver, and on they went once more.

Toad was almost himself again by now. He sat up, looked about him, and he turned to the driver at his side.

'Please, sir,' he said, 'I wish you would kindly let me try and drive the car for a little. I've been watching you carefully, and it looks so easy and so interesting, and I should like to be able to tell my friends that once I had driven a motor-car!'

The driver laughed at the proposal, so heartily that the gentleman inquired what the matter was. When he heard, he said, to Toad's delight, 'Bravo, ma'am! I like your spirit. Let her have a try, and look after her. She won't do any harm.'

Toad eagerly scrambled into the seat vacated by the driver, took the steering-wheel in his hands, listened with affected humility to the instructions given him, and set the car in motion, but very slowly and carefully at first, for he was determined to be prudent.

The gentlemen behind clapped their hands and applauded, and Toad heard them saying, 'How well she does it! Fancy a washerwoman driving a car as well as that, the first time!'

Toad went a little faster, then faster still, and faster.

He heard the gentlemen call out warningly, 'Be careful, washerwoman!' And this annoyed him, and he began to lose his head.

The driver tried to interfere, but he pinned him down in his seat with one elbow, and put on full speed. The rush of air in his face, the hum of the engine, and the light jump of the car beneath him intoxicated his weak brain. 'Washerwoman, indeed!' he shouted recklessly. 'Ho, ho! I am the Toad, the motor-car snatcher, the prison-breaker, the Toad who always escapes! Sit still, and you shall know what driving really is, for you are in the hands of the famous, the skilful, the entirely fearless Toad!'

With a cry of horror the whole party rose and flung themselves on him. 'Seize him!' they cried, 'seize the Toad, the wicked animal who stole our motor-car! Bind him, chain him, drag him to the nearest police-station! Down with the desperate and dangerous Toad!'

Alas! They should have remembered to stop the motor-car before playing any pranks of that sort. With a half-turn of the wheel the Toad sent the car crashing through the low hedge that ran along the road-side. One mighty bound, a violent shock, and the wheels of the car were churning up the thick mud of a horse-pond.

Toad found himself flying through the air with the strong upward rush and delicate curve of a swallow, then he landed on his back with a thump, in the soft rich grass of a meadow. Sitting up, he could just see the motor-car in the pond, nearly submerged; the gentlemen and the driver, encumbered by their long coats, were floundering helplessly in the water.

He picked himself up rapidly and set off running across country as hard as he could, scrambling through hedges, jumping ditches, pounding across fields, till he was breathless and weary, and had to settle down into an easy walk. When he had recovered his breath somewhat, and was able to think calmly, he laughed till he had to sit down under a hedge. 'Ho, ho!' he cried, in ecstasies of self-admiration. 'Toad again! Toad, as usual, comes out on the top! Who was it got them to give him a lift? Who managed to get on the front seat for the sake of fresh air? Who persuaded them into letting him see if he could drive? Who landed them all in a horse-pond? Why, Toad, of course; clever Toad, great Toad, *good* Toad! O, how clever I am! How clever, how clever, how very clev –'

A slight noise at a distance behind him made him turn his head and look. O horror! O misery! O despair!

About two fields off, a chauffeur in his leather gaiters and two large rural policemen were visible, running towards him as hard as they could go!

Poor Toad sprang to his feet and pelted away again, his heart in his mouth. 'O my!' he gasped, as he panted along, 'what an *ass* I am! What a *conceited* and heedless ass! Swaggering again! Sitting still and gassing again! O my! O my! O my!'

He glanced back, and saw to his dismay that they were gaining on him. On he ran desperately, but kept looking back, and saw that they still gained steadily. He did his best, but he was a fat animal, and his legs were short, and still they gained. He could hear them close behind him now. Ceasing to heed where he was going, he struggled on blindly and wildly, looking back over his shoulder at the now triumphant enemy, when suddenly the earth failed under his feet, he grasped at the air, and, splash! he found himself head over ears in deep water, and he knew that in his blind panic he had run straight into the river!

He rose to the surface and tried to grasp the reeds and the rushes that grew along the water's edge close under the bank, but the stream was so strong that it tore them out of his hands. 'O my!' gasped poor Toad, 'if ever I steal a motor-car again!' – then down he went, and came up breathless and spluttering. Presently he saw that he was approaching a big dark hole in the bank, just above his head, and as the stream bore him past he reached up with a paw and caught hold of the edge and held on. Then slowly and with difficulty he drew himself up out of the water, till at last he was able to rest his elbows on the edge of the hole. There he remained for some minutes, puffing and panting, for he was quite exhausted.

As he sighed and blew and stared before him into the dark hole, some bright small thing shone and twinkled in its depths, moving towards him. As it approached, a face grew up gradually around it, and it was a familiar face!

Brown and small, with whiskers.

Grave and round, with neat ears and silky hair.

It was the Water Rat!

Cheer Up, Toad!

The Rat put out a neat little brown paw, gripped Toad firmly by the scruff of the neck, gave a great hoist and a pull, and the water-logged Toad came up slowly but surely over the edge of the hole, till at last he stood safe and sound in the hall.

'O Ratty!' he cried. 'I've been through such times since I saw you last, you can't think! Such trials, such sufferings, and all so nobly borne! Then such escapes, such disguises, and all so cleverly planned and carried out! Been in prison – got out of it, of course! Been thrown into a canal – swam ashore! Stole a horse – sold him for a large sum of money! Humbugged everybody – made 'em all do exactly what I wanted! O, I *am* a smart Toad, and no mistake! What do you think my last exploit was? Just hold on till I tell you –'

'Toad,' said the Water Rat, gravely and firmly, 'you go off upstairs at once, and take off that old cotton rag and clean yourself thoroughly, and put on some of my clothes, and try and come down looking like a gentleman if you *can*; for a more shabby, bedraggled, disreputable-looking object than you are I never set eyes on in my whole life! Now, stop swaggering and arguing, and be off! I'll have something to say to you later!'

Toad was at first inclined to stop and do some talking back at him. However, he caught sight of himself in the looking-glass over the hat-stand, with the rusty black bonnet perched rakishly over one eye, and he changed his mind and went very quickly and humbly upstairs to the Rat's dressing-room. There he had a thorough wash and brush-up, changed his clothes, and stood for a long time before the glass, contemplating himself with pride and pleasure, and thinking what utter idiots all the people must have been to have ever mistaken him for one moment for a washerwoman.

By the time he came down again luncheon was on the table, and very glad Toad was to see it, for he had been through some trying experiences and had taken much hard exercise since the excellent breakfast provided for him by the gipsy.

While they ate Toad told the Rat all his adventures, dwelling chiefly on his own cleverness. But the more he talked and boasted, the more grave and silent the Rat became.

When at last Toad had talked himself to a standstill, there was silence for a while, and then the Rat said, 'Now, Toady, I don't want to give you pain, after all you've been through already, but don't you see what an awful ass you've been making of yourself? You know that you've never had anything but trouble from motor-cars from the moment you first set eyes on one. But if you *will* be mixed up with them – why *steal* them? When are you going to be sensible, and think of your friends, and try and be a credit to them?'

Now Toad was a thoroughly good-hearted animal, and never minded being jawed by those who were his real friends, so when the Rat had quite finished, he heaved a deep sigh and said, very nicely and humbly, 'Quite right, Ratty! How *sound* you always are! Yes, I've been a conceited old ass, I can quite see that, but now I'm going to be a good Toad, and not do it any more. As for motor-cars, I've not been at all so keen about them since my last ducking in that river of yours. The fact is, while I was hanging on to the edge of your hole and getting my breath, I had a sudden idea – a really brilliant idea – connected with motor-boats. There, there! don't take on so, old chap, and stamp, and upset things; it was only an idea, and we won't talk any more about it now. We'll have our coffee and a quiet chat, and then I'm going to stroll gently down to Toad Hall, and get into clothes of my own, and set things going again on the old lines.'

'Stroll gently down to Toad Hall?' cried the Rat, greatly excited. 'What are you talking about? Do you mean to say you haven't *heard*?'

'Heard what?' said Toad, turning rather pale. 'Go on, Ratty! Quick! Don't spare me! What haven't I heard?'

'Do you mean to tell me,' shouted the Rat, thumping with his little fist upon the table, 'that you've heard nothing about the Stoats and Weasels and how they've been and taken Toad Hall?'

Toad leaned his elbows on the table, and his chin on his paws, and a large tear welled up in each of his eyes, overflowed and splashed on the table, plop! plop!

'Go on, Ratty,' he murmured presently; 'tell me all. I can bear it.'

'When you – got – into that – that – trouble of yours,' said the Rat, 'well, it was a good deal talked about down here, naturally, not only along the riverside, but even in the Wild Wood. Animals took sides, as always happens. The River-bankers stuck up for you, but the Wild Wood animals got very cocky, and went about saying you were done for this time! You would never come back again, never, never!'

Toad nodded once more, keeping silence.

'That's the sort of little beasts they are,' the Rat went on. 'But Mole and Badger, they stuck out, through thick and thin, that you would come back again soon, somehow. They didn't know exactly how, but somehow! So they arranged to move their things into Toad Hall, and sleep there, and keep it aired, and have it all ready for you when you turned up.

'Now I come to the most painful and tragic part of my story. One dark night – it was a *very* dark night, and blowing hard, too, and raining simply cats and dogs – a band of stoats and weasels, armed to the teeth, crept silently up the carriage-drive. The Mole and the Badger were sitting by the fire in the smoking-room, telling stories and suspecting nothing, when those bloodthirsty villains broke down the doors and rushed in upon them from every side. They made the best fight they could, but what was the good? They were unarmed, and taken by surprise, and what can two animals do against hundreds? They took and beat them severely with sticks, those two poor faithful creatures, and turned them out into the cold and the wet, with many insulting and uncalled-for remarks!'

Here the unfeeling Toad broke into a snigger, and then pulled himself together and tried to look particularly solemn.

'And the Wild Wooders have been living in Toad Hall ever since,' continued the Rat, 'and going on simply anyhow! Lying in bed half the day, and breakfast at all hours, and the place in such a mess (I'm told) it's not fit to be seen! Eating your grub, and drinking your drink, and making bad jokes about you. And they're telling the tradespeople and everybody that they've come to stay for good.'

'O, have they!' said Toad, getting up and seizing a stick. 'I'll jolly soon see about that!'

'It's no good, Toad!' called the Rat after him. 'You'd better come back and sit down; you'll only get into trouble.'

But the Toad was off, and there was no hold-
ing him. He marched rapidly down the road, his
stick over his shoulder, fuming and muttering to
himself in his anger, till he got near his front gate,
when suddenly there popped up from behind the
palings a long yellow ferret with a gun.

'Who comes there?' said the ferret sharply.

'Stuff and nonsense!' said Toad very angrily.
'What do you mean by talking like that to me?
Come out of it at once, or I'll —'

The ferret said never a word, but he brought
his gun up to his shoulder. Toad prudently dropped flat in the road, and *Bang!* a bullet whistled
over his head.

The startled Toad scrambled to his feet and scampered off down the road as hard as he could; and as he ran he heard the ferret laughing, and other horrid thin little laughs taking it up and carrying on the sound.

He went back, very crestfallen, and told the Water Rat.

'What did I tell you?' said the Rat. 'It's no good. They've got sentries posted, and they are all armed. You must just wait until we have seen the Mole and the Badger, and heard their latest news, and held conference and taken their advice in this difficult matter.'

'O, ah, yes, of course, the Mole and the Badger,' said Toad lightly. 'What's become of them, the dear fellows? I had forgotten all about them.'

'Well may you ask!' said the Rat reproachfully. 'While you were riding about the country in expensive motor-cars, and galloping proudly on blood-horses, and breakfasting on the fat of the land, those two poor devoted animals have been camping out in the open, in every sort of weather, living very rough by day and lying very hard by night, watching over your house, patrolling your boundaries, keeping a constant eye on the stoats and the weasels, scheming and planning and contriving how to get your property back for you. You don't deserve to have such true and loyal friends, Toad, you don't, really. Some day, when it's too late, you'll be sorry you didn't value them more while you had them!'

They had just finished their supper and resumed their arm-chairs, when there came a heavy knock at the door.

Toad was nervous, but the Rat, nodding mysteriously at him, went straight up to the door and opened it, and in walked Mr Badger.

He had all the appearance of one who for some nights had been kept away from home and all its little comforts and conveniences. His shoes were covered with mud, and he was looking very rough and tousled; but then he had never been a very smart man, the Badger, at the best of times. He came solemnly up to Toad, shook him by the paw, and said, 'Welcome home, Toad! Alas! what am I saying? Home, indeed! This is a poor home-coming. Unhappy Toad!' Then he turned his back on him, sat down to the table, drew his chair up, and helped himself to a large slice of cold pie.

Presently there came another and a lighter knock and Rat ushered in the Mole, very shabby and unwashed, with bits of hay and straw sticking in his fur.

'Hooray! Here's old Toad!' cried the Mole, his face beaming. 'Fancy having you back again!' And he began to dance round him. 'We never dreamt you would turn up so soon! Why, you must have managed to escape, you clever, ingenious, intelligent Toad! Supposing you talk while I eat. Not a bite since breakfast! O my! O my!' And he sat down at the supper table and helped himself liberally to cold beef and pickles.

Afterwards they held their council of war.

'The position's about as bad as it can be,' said
the Mole grumpily, 'and as for what's to be done,
why, blest if I know! The Badger and I have been
round and round the place, by night and by day;
always the same thing. Sentries posted everywhere, guns poked out at us, stones thrown at us;
always an animal on the look-out, and when
they see us, my! how they do laugh! That's what
annoys me most!'

Then the Badger spoke. 'What the Mole says
is quite true. The stoats are on guard, at every
point, and they make the best sentinels in the
world. It's quite useless to think of attacking the
place. They're too strong for us.'

'Then it's all over,' sobbed the Toad, crying
into the sofa cushions. 'I shall go and enlist for

a soldier, and never see my dear Toad Hall any more!'

'Come, cheer up, Toady!' said the Badger. 'There are more ways of getting back a place than taking it by storm. I haven't said my last word yet. Now I'm going to tell you a great secret.'

Toad sat up slowly and dried his eyes. Secrets had an immense attraction for him.

'There – is – an – underground – passage,' said the Badger impressively, 'that leads from the river bank quite near here, right up into the middle of Toad Hall.'

'O, nonsense! Badger,' said Toad rather airily. 'You've been listening to some of the yarns they spin in the public-houses about here. I know every inch of Toad Hall, inside and out. Nothing of the sort, I do assure you!'

'My young friend,' said the Badger with great severity, 'your father, who was a worthy animal – a lot worthier than some others I know – was a particular friend of mine, and told me a great deal he wouldn't have dreamt of telling you. He discovered that passage – he didn't make it, of course; that was done hundreds of years before he ever came to live there – and he repaired it and cleaned it out, because he thought it might come in useful some day, in case of trouble or danger, and he showed it to me. "Don't let my son know about it," he said. "He's a good boy, but very light and volatile in character, and simply cannot hold his tongue. If he's ever in a real fix, and it would be of use to him, you may tell him about the secret passage, but not before."'

The other animals looked hard at Toad to see how he would take it. Toad was inclined to be sulky at first, but he brightened up immediately, like the good fellow he was.

'Well, well,' he said; 'perhaps I am a bit of a talker. A popular fellow such as I am – my tongue gets wagging. Never mind. Go on, Badger. How's this passage of yours going to help us?'

'I've found out a thing or two lately,' continued the Badger. 'There's going to be a big banquet tomorrow night. It's somebody's birthday – the Chief Weasel's, I believe – and all the weasels will be gathered together in the dining-hall, eating and drinking and laughing and carrying on, suspecting nothing. No guns, no swords, no sticks, no arms of any sort whatever!'

'But the sentinels will be posted as usual,' remarked the Rat.

'Exactly,' said the Badger; 'that is my point. The weasels will trust entirely to their excellent sentinels, the stoats. And that is where the passage comes in. That very useful tunnel leads right up under the butler's pantry, next to the dining-hall!'

'Aha! that squeaky board in the butler's pantry!' said Toad. 'Now I understand it!'

'We shall creep out quietly into the butler's pantry –' cried the Mole.

'– with our pistols and swords and sticks –' shouted the Rat.

'– and rush in upon them,' said the Badger.

'– and whack 'em, and whack 'em, and whack 'em!' cried the Toad in ecstasy, running round and round the room, and jumping over the chairs.

'Very well, then,' said the Badger, resuming his usual dry manner, 'our plan is settled, and there's nothing more for you to argue and squabble about. So, as it's getting very late, all of you go right off to bed at once. We will make all the necessary arrangements in the course of the morning tomorrow.'

II

The Attack

Toad slept till a late hour next morning, and by
the time he got down he found that the other
animals had finished their breakfast some time
before. The Badger sat in the arm-chair, reading
the paper, and not concerning himself in the
slightest about what was going to happen that
very evening, while the Mole drew his arm
through Toad's, led him out into the open air,
and made him tell all his adventures from beginning to end, which Toad was only too willing to
do. The Rat, on the other hand, was running
around the room busily, with his arms full of
weapons of every kind, distributing them in four
little heaps on the floor, and saying excitedly
under his breath, as he ran, 'Here's-a-sword-for-
the-Rat, here's-a-sword-for-the-Mole, here's-
a-sword-for-the-Toad, here's-a-sword-for-the-

Badger! Here's-a-pistol-for-the-Rat, here's-a-pistol-for-the-Mole, here's-a-pistol-for-the-Toad, here's-a-pistol-for-the-Badger!' And so on, in a regular, rhythmical way, while the four little heaps gradually grew and grew.

Later, when it began to grow dark, the Rat, with an air of excitement and mystery, summoned his friends back into the parlour, stood each of them up alongside of his little heap, and proceeded to dress them up for the coming expedition. He was very earnest and thorough-going about it, and the affair took quite a long time. First, there was a belt to go round each animal, and then a sword to be stuck into each belt, and then a cutlass on the other side to balance it. Then a pair of pistols, a policeman's truncheon, several sets of handcuffs, some bandages and sticking-plaster, and a flask and a sandwich-case. The Badger laughed good-humouredly and said, 'All right, Ratty! It amuses you and it doesn't hurt me. I'm going to do all I've got to do with this here stick.' But the Rat only said, '*Please*, Badger! You know I shouldn't like you to blame me afterwards and say I had forgotten *anything*!'

When all was quite ready, the Badger took a dark lantern in one paw, grasped his great stick with the other, and said, 'Now then, follow me!

Mole first; Rat next; Toad last. And look here,
Toady! Don't you chatter so much as usual, or
you'll be sent back, as sure as fate!'

The Toad was so anxious not to be left out that
he took up the inferior position assigned to him
without a murmur, and the animals set off. The
Badger led them along by the river for a little
way, and then suddenly swung himself over the
edge into a hole in the river bank, a little above
the water. The Mole and the Rat followed
silently, swinging themselves successfully into
the hole as they had seen the Badger do; but when
it came to Toad's turn, of course, he managed to
slip and fall into the water with a loud splash and
a squeal of alarm. He was hauled out by his
friends, rubbed down and wrung out hastily,

comforted, and set on his legs; but the Badger was seriously angry, and told him that the very next time he made a fool of himself he would most certainly be left behind.

So at last they were in the secret passage, and the cutting-out expedition had really begun!

It was cold, and dark, and damp, and low, and narrow, and poor Toad began to shiver, partly from dread of what might be before him, partly because he was wet through. The lantern was far ahead, and he could not help lagging behind a little in the darkness. Then he heard the Rat call out warningly, '*Come* on, Toad!' and a terror seized him of being left behind, alone in the darkness, and he 'came on' with such a rush that he upset the Rat into the Mole and the Mole into the Badger, and for a moment all was confusion. The Badger thought they were being attacked from behind, and, as there was no room to use a stick or a cutlass, drew a pistol, and was on the point of putting a bullet into Toad. When he found out what had really happened he was very angry indeed, and said, 'Now this time that tiresome Toad *shall* be left behind!'

But Toad whimpered, and the other two promised that they would be answerable for his good conduct, and at last the Badger was pacified, and the procession moved on; only this time the Rat brought up the rear, with a firm grip on the shoulder of Toad.

So they groped and shuffled along, with their ears pricked up and their paws on their pistols, till at last the Badger said, 'We ought by now to be pretty nearly under the Hall.'

Then suddenly they heard, far away as it might be, and yet apparently nearly over their heads, a confused murmur of sound, as if people were shouting and cheering and stamping on the floor and hammering on tables. The Toad's nervous terrors all returned, but the Badger only remarked placidly, 'They *are* going it, the weasels!'

The passage now began to slope upwards; they groped onward a little further, and then the noise broke out again, quite distinct this time, and very close above them. 'Ooo-ray-oo-ray-oo-ray-ooray!' they heard, and the stamping of little feet on the floor, and the clinking of glasses as little fists pounded on the table. '*What* a time they're having!' said the Badger. 'Come on!' They hurried along the passage till it came to a full stop, and they found themselves standing under the trap-door that led up into the butler's pantry.

Such a tremendous noise was going on in the banqueting-hall that there was little danger of their being overheard. The Badger said, 'Now, boys, all together!' and the four of them put their shoulders to the trap-door and heaved it back. Hoisting each other up, they found themselves standing in the pantry, with only a door between them and the banqueting-hall, where their enemies were carousing.

The noise, as they emerged from the passage, was simply deafening. At last, as the cheering and hammering slowly subsided, a voice could be made out saying, 'Well, I do not propose to detain you much longer' – (great applause) – 'but before I resume my seat' – (renewed cheering) – 'I should like to say one word about our kind host, Mr Toad. We all know Toad!' – (great laughter) – '*Good* Toad, *modest* Toad, *honest* Toad!' – (shrieks of merriment).

'Only just let me get at him!' muttered Toad, grinding his teeth.

'Hold hard a minute!' said the Badger, restraining him with difficulty. 'Get ready, all of you!'

'– Let me sing you a little song,' went on the voice, 'which I have composed on the subject of Toad' – (prolonged applause).

Then the Chief Weasel – for it was he – began in a high, squeaky voice:

> Toad he went a-pleasuring
> Gaily down the street –

The Badger drew himself up, took a firm grip of his stick with both paws, glanced round at his comrades and cried:

'The hour is come! Follow me!'

And flung the door open wide.

My!

What a squealing and a squeaking and a screeching filled the air!

Well might the terrified weasels dive under the tables and spring madly up at the windows! Well might the ferrets rush wildly for the fireplace and get hopelessly jammed in the chimney! Well might tables and chairs be upset, and glass and china be sent crashing on the floor, in the panic of that terrible moment when the four Heroes strode wrathfully into the room! The mighty Badger, his whiskers bristling, his great cudgel whistling through the air; Mole, black and grim, brandishing his stick and shouting his awful war-cry, 'A Mole! A Mole!'; Rat, desperate and determined, his belt bulging with weapons of every age and every variety; Toad, frenzied with excitement and injured pride, swollen to twice his ordinary size, leaping into the air and emitting Toad-whoops that chilled them to the marrow! 'Toad he went a-pleasuring!' he yelled. 'I'll pleasure 'em!' and he went straight for the Chief Weasel. They were but four in all, but to the panic-stricken weasels the hall seemed full of monstrous animals, grey, black, brown, and yellow, whooping and flourishing enormous

cudgels; and they broke and fled with squeals of terror and dismay, this way and that, through the windows, up the chimney, anywhere to get out of reach of those terrible sticks.

The affair was soon over. Up and down, the whole length of the hall, strode the four friends, whacking with their sticks at every head that showed itself, and in five minutes the room was cleared. Through the broken windows the shrieks of terrified weasels escaping across the lawn were borne faintly to their ears; on the floor lay prostrate some dozen or so of the enemy, on whom the Mole was busily engaged in fitting handcuffs. The Badger, resting from his labours, leant on his stick and wiped his honest brow.

'Mole,' he said, 'you're the best of fellows! Just cut along outside and look after those stoat-sentries. I've an idea that we shan't have much trouble from *them* tonight!'

The Mole vanished promptly through a window, and the Badger bade the other two set a table on its legs again, pick up knives and forks and plates and glasses from the debris on the floor, and see if they could find materials for a supper. 'I want some grub, I do,' he said, in that rather common way he had of speaking. 'Stir your stumps, Toad, and look lively! We've got your house back for you, and you don't offer us so much as a sandwich.'

Toad felt rather hurt that the Badger didn't say pleasant things to him, as he had to the Mole, and tell him what a fine fellow he was, and how splendidly he had fought, for he was rather particularly pleased with himself and the way he had gone for the Chief Weasel and sent him flying across the table with one blow of his stick. But he bustled about, and so did the Rat, and soon they found some guava jelly in a glass dish, and a cold chicken, a tongue that had hardly been touched, some trifle, and quite a lot of lobster salad, and in the pantry they came upon a basketful of French rolls and any quantity of cheese, butter, and celery. They were just about to sit down when the Mole clambered in through the window, chuckling, with an armful of rifles.

'It's all over,' he reported. 'From what I can make out, as soon as the stoats heard the shrieks and the yells and the uproar inside the hall, some of them threw down their rifles and fled. The others stood fast for a bit, but when the weasels came rushing out upon them they thought they were betrayed, and the stoats grappled with the weasels, and the weasels fought to get away, and they wrestled and wriggled and punched each other, and rolled over and over, till most of 'em rolled into the river! They've all disappeared by now, one way or another, and I've got their rifles. So *that's* all right!'

'Excellent and deserving animal!' said the Badger, his mouth full of chicken and trifle. 'Now, there's just one more thing I want you to do, Mole, before you sit down to your supper along of us, and I wouldn't trouble you only I know I can trust you to see a thing done, and I wish I could say the same of everyone I know. I'd send Rat, if he wasn't a poet. I want you to take those fellows on the floor there upstairs with you, and have some bedrooms cleaned out and tidied up and made really comfortable. See that they sweep *under* the beds, and put clean sheets and pillow-cases on, and turn down one corner of the bed-clothes, just as you know it ought to be done, and have a can of hot water, and clean towels, and fresh cakes of soap, put in each room. And then you can give them a licking apiece, if it's any satisfaction to you, and put them out by the back

door, and we shan't see any more of *them*, I
fancy. And then come along and have some of
this cold tongue. It's first-rate. I'm very pleased
with you, Mole!'

The good-natured Mole picked up a stick,
formed his prisoners up in a line on the floor,
gave them the order 'Quick march!' and led his
squad off to the upper floor. After a time, he
appeared again, smiling, and said that every
room was ready, and as clean as a new pin. 'And
I didn't have to lick them, either,' he added. 'I
thought, on the whole, they had had licking
enough for one night, and the weasels, when I put
the point to them, quite agreed with me, and said
they wouldn't think of troubling me. They were
very penitent, and said they were extremely sorry

for what they had done, but it was all the fault of the Chief Weasel and the stoats, and if ever they could do anything for us at any time to make up, we had only got to mention it. So I gave them a roll apiece, and let them out at the back, and off they ran, as hard as they could!'

Then the Mole pulled his chair up to the table, and pitched into the cold tongue, and Toad, like the gentleman he was, put all his jealousy from him, and said heartily, 'Thank you kindly, dear Mole, for all your pains and trouble tonight, and especially for your cleverness this morning!' The Badger was pleased at that, and said, 'There spoke my brave Toad!' So they finished their supper in great joy and contentment, and presently retired to rest between clean sheets, safe in Toad's ancestral home, won back by matchless valour, consummate strategy, and a proper handling of sticks.